When Two's Not Enough

"Tribal Fusion" -- Whenever and wherever he dances, Dominic collects propositions, but the Lady Lenore's proposal takes him by surprise.

"Two Brothers" -- A divorcée in a flashy sports car attracts the attention of two young virgin brothers visiting the "big" city of Boise.

"Honeymoon" -- Although she expected to honeymoon aboard a cruise ship, Allison finds herself sailing on a private yacht staffed by an incredibly beautiful couple. Believing her new husband wants to hide his older, less attractive wife, makes it difficult to enjoy the hedonistic delights offered in paradise.

"Jail Bait" -- Serena wants Joshua to pop her cherry, but he won't touch her because of her age. When her birthday finally makes it legal, he arranges for a very special celebration.

"Nikki's Birthday" -- Even someone happy in a monogamous relationship might find the gift of a hot, new toy for an evening of decadence incredibly exciting.

"Market Boy" -- When a beautiful Domme offers Jack the opportunity to serve at a party for her friends, he responds too quickly and too eagerly, getting more than he bargained for.

"The Cougar and the College Boys" -- Alone in the woods, hours from Portland, Tess discovers four college friends staying in a nearby cabin. The boys invite her to share their campfire, their dinner, and ...

I.G. Frederick trades words for cash, specializing in erotic fiction and poetry since 2001. Her erotic short stories appear in Hustler Fantasies, Forum, Foreplay, and Desire Presents, as well as electronic, audio, and print anthologies. Her novels receive high praise from readers, critics, and other authors.

A FemDom, Ms. Frederick, owns the man she adores. Although dominant in the rest of his life, he demonstrates his love by serving as her submissive. Ms. Frederick often writes about finding love in BDSM relationships from the authority of one enjoying that for almost a decade.

http://eroticawriter.net/

When Two's Not Enough

Seven sexy ménage stories

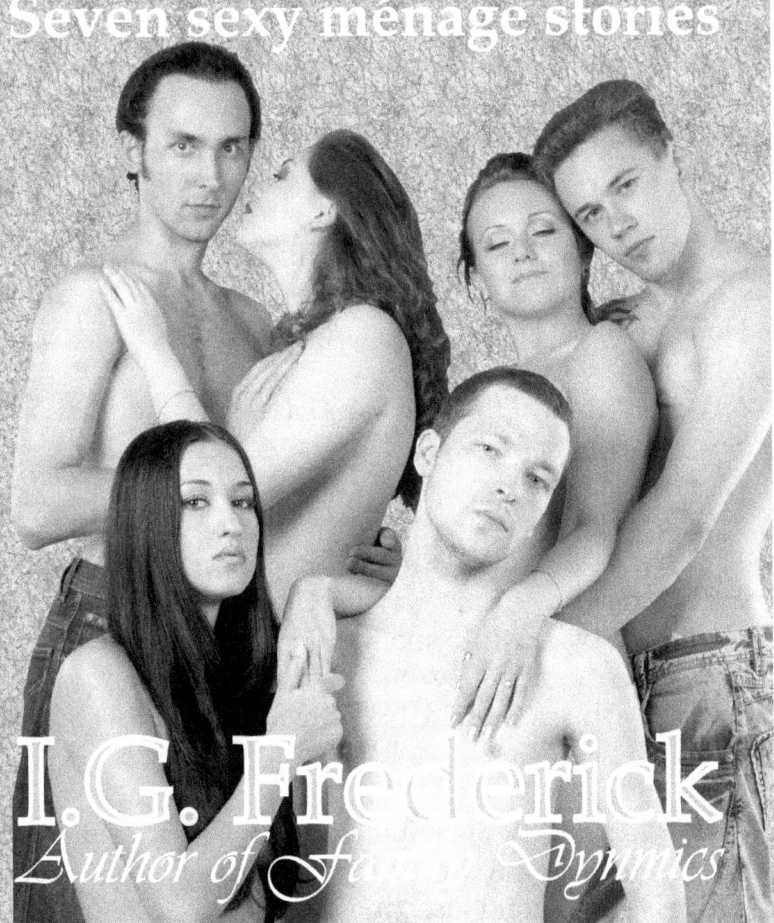

I.G. Frederick

Author of Family Dynamics

When Two's Not Enough
© **2014 by I.G. Frederick**

ISBN: 978-1937471-21-7

Pussy Cat Press
http://pussycatpress.com/publisher.html/
P.O. Box 19764
Portland OR 97280

First published electronically in 2012

"Two Brothers" first published in Blue Moon's *MILF Anthology: Twenty-One Steamy Stories*, June 2006
"Honeymoon" first published by Ravenous Romance, Dec., 2008
"Nikki's Birthday" first published as Slave's Birthday Treat, *Mammoth Book of Erotic Confessions*, May, 2009 and also appears in *Mammoth Book of Quick and Dirty Erotica*, April, 2013

Table of Contents

Tribal Fusion

By I.G. Frederick

My jaw dropped as the belly dancer lowered himself closer to the floor, his back parallel to the boards, supported only by powerful legs hidden in billowing pants. His shoulder-length braids swept the stage. When he moved, wide metal bracelets on both arms clinked together loudly enough to be heard above the beat of the drums. Strands of beads and feathers crisscrossed his bare chest, additional bangles encircled his biceps, and he had several scarves tied around his narrow hips.

I stared, mesmerized, while he undulated back to a standing position and continued dancing. His belly rippled as he threw his hips from one side to the other in rapid movements almost too fast to track. He towered over the three female belly dancers who stood in a half circle watching his solo. When he finished, everyone in the bar stood up in unison and the applause and zaghareet lasted almost five minutes.

As soon as the crowd settled down, I signaled a waitress

and asked her to buy the man a drink and put it on my tab. When she spoke to him, he glanced my way. Using my feet, I pushed out the empty chair across from me and pointed to it with my palm facing him. He grinned, spoke to the waitress, and approached our table. Even just walking, he moved with a sensual grace. Long and lean, he had almost no body hair and just a tease of a beard on his face. A sheen of sweat covered his toffee-colored skin.

When I extended my hand, palm down, he caught my fingers across his and lifted them just close enough to his lips that I could feel the heat. He lowered himself into the chair just as the waitress brought him a pint of stout and he lifted the mug toward me before taking a long, slow pull.

"I'm Dominic. I hope this means you enjoyed our performance."

"I'm Lady Lenore and this is my submissive, Stan."

The two men shook hands.

"I enjoyed your part in it tremendously. We have belly dancers in here every month, but I've never seen a male perform before. How long have you been dancing?"

"Since college when I saw a production of Arabian Nights and fell in love with the dance form."

I smiled. "That didn't exactly answer my question."

"Not the one you articulated perhaps." His dark brown eyes twinkled. "I'm teaching a workshop at the college tomorrow afternoon. Perhaps you, or your," he stared Stan up and down, "submissive would care to take a class?"

I laughed. "I don't think either of us is cut out for those kind of movements. Besides, I'm more interested in the instructor than his class."

"Oh?" He set his half empty mug on the table and leaned forward. "In what way?"

I rested my hands on the table in front of me and whispered in his ear. "My boy here's a cuckold."

Dominic sat back in his chair. He stared at me and then at Stan and then back at me.

"Ma'am. I've had many interesting offers on my travels, but I must admit that's a first."

"He's also quite good with his mouth if you're interested." I gave Stan a look and he made an O with his mouth and extended his tongue until it touched the tip of his nose.

"I need to clean up..."

"Don't bother. Stan can bathe you at my place. Why don't you just get your things."

Dominic blinked for a few seconds. Then he downed the rest of his beer and rose to his feet. "I'll be right back."

"Meet us outside in the parking lot. I have a red Mustang convertible."

"Of course you do." He grinned displaying white teeth against his dark skin. "I'll be out front in ten minutes."

I settled the bill and left the bar, waving to a couple of acquaintances but not stopping to chat. Stan opened the passenger door for me and I had him get into the driver's seat long enough to lower the rag top. Dominic approached the car carrying a brown leather satchel. Stan took it and stashed it in the trunk while Dominic folded his long legs into the back of the car.

Stan knew to take a circuitous route to the house, so it took almost twenty minutes. I sat with my back to the door both so I could enjoy the discomfort Stan tried to hide beneath a stoic expression and so I could talk to Dominic. I learned he'd been on tour for almost a year, performing what he called "tribal fusion rooted in Egyptian style." Apparently, he wasn't picky about where he danced: theaters, street fairs, ethnic and cultural festivals, restaurants, bookstores, bars, and lingerie shops had all welcomed him. He was even available to hire for birthdays and weddings. I wondered if I could get him to come back to town for a play party.

When Stan pulled into the garage, Dominic jumped over the side of the car and opened my door before Stan could turn off the engine. Stan clambered out. Although several inches shorter than Dominic, he's still over six feet tall, which is why I have a Mustang and not a BMW. He extracted Dominic's bag from the trunk and both men followed me into the house. Dominic and I waited while Stan stripped.

"He's not allowed to wear clothing in the house," I explained.

"I see." Dominic observed Stan's muscular body, much stockier than his own, with what might have been admiration. Or perhaps, he was just deciding how far he was willing to indulge me. One eyebrow rose above the other for a few minutes as he stared at the metal tube encasing Stan's cock.

"Would you like anything to drink?"

"Just water, thanks."

"With or without ice?" Stan asked. "Sparkling or flat?"

"Flat with ice."

"Bring it upstairs." I started up the curving staircase. "This way," I said to Dominic.

He kicked off his sneakers and grabbed his bag.

"You can leave that. Stan will bring it."

"No problem." Dominic followed me up the stairs and I heard a sharp intake of breath when I led him into the master suite.

"Why don't you take all that off, so Stan can give you a proper bath." I led the way into the marble and gold bathroom that was bigger than my first apartment. I lowered myself into my leather-covered boudoir chair, strategically placed in the corner so I could see everything in the three-person whirlpool tub and the glass-enclosed shower that stretched along one wall.

Stan had found some Middle Eastern music in my collection and started playing it on the house stereo just as Dominic reached for the knot that held one of his scarves in place. His hips moved slowly and he turned around, pulling the scarf off as he did. One by one first the scarves and then the beads found their way to the floor while Dominic's hips continued their sultry swaying.

By then, Stan had found his way to the bathroom and he pulled each piece of discarded clothing away before Dominic could step on it. I crossed my legs, his performance having more of an impact on me than I'd realized. When only his billowing chalwar remained, Dominic unbuttoned the fastenings and flung his hips from side to side until the fabric pooled at his feet. He wore tight black underpants that couldn't hide an obvious bulge. Slowly, he eased them down his hips and I licked my lips. Hanging from his triangle of dark, bristly hair was a cock as long and lean as the man. I wonder if it got even longer when erect, or, I could hope, thicker.

Stan crawled over to the tub and turned the taps. "How hot do you like it, Sir?"

Dominic kicked his pants and underwear behind him. "Steaming." He swallowed the water in the glass that Stan had set on the marble tile of the two-foot wide tub surround.

Stan produced a bamboo tray covered with a variety of bottles and bars. Dominic selected sandalwood soap, handed it to Stan, and stepped into the tub. Steam poured from the water spilling from the tap and billowed around Dominic's knees. Stan unwrapped the soap and followed Dominic into the tub, easing himself down to his knees in the hot water.

He wet the bar and slid it slowly up and down first one of Dominic's calves, then the other. That magnificent cock twitched just a bit and I smiled. Stan worked his way up Dominic's thighs and then swirled the bar across his ass. I squirmed. After re-wetting the bar, Stan soaped up Dominic's pubic hair and to my delight his cock rose and thickened. Oh, so slowly, Stan dragged the bar up and down Dominic's engorged cock, licking his lips in anticipation. My panties were getting soaked.

Dominic's eyes were closed and he swayed just a little to the rhythm of the music as if he couldn't resist the drumbeat. He lowered himself into the hot water, which now came up to his nipples, and Stan continued applying soap to his chest, arms, and neck. When Dominic eased himself back to float in the hot water, Stan worked his way around so he could massage soap into Dominic's scalp.

Dominic smiled. "Will you join us, my lady?"

"No, but when you're clean, I'll expect *you* to join me in the bedroom."

"My pleasure, Ma'am." He sat up and Stan switched off the taps, opened the drain, and reached for the hand shower. He rinsed Dominic's hair and then his arms and chest. Dominic stood and Stan rinsed his pubes and legs, then rinsed himself. The two men stepped out onto the plush mat. Stan grabbed a thick towel and rubbed Dominic's kinky hair dry. As he worked his way down, he knelt at the taller man's feet. He stared at the thick cock that almost poked him in the eye, then at me. I nodded and Stan looked up at Dominic who nodded as well.

My breathing grew heavier as I watched Stan lick the foreskin before pulling it back to expose the glans. Dominic gasped as Stan encircled the tip with his tongue. Several of my lovers have reported that Stan is quite good and apparently Dominic agreed. For the first time since he arrived at the house, he stood perfectly still, allowing Stan to swallow as much of his cock as he could. Stan struggled to take more in, relaxing his throat until he got his nose into Dominic's pubes. I could hear both of them breathing in time to the drums.

I rose and walked over to Dominic, caressing his lovely, muscular ass with my palm. He twisted at the waist, without giving up an inch of Stan's mouth, and pulled me close with one arm. The scent of sandalwood permeated my nostrils as he pressed his soft lips against mine. I ran my tongue between them and pushed into the moist cavern of his mouth, enjoying the coffee aftertaste of the stout. He met my tongue with his own and they danced together inside his mouth while he slipped the straps of my dress off my shoulders.

With only one hand, he managed to get my bra unclasped, never releasing my waist with the other. He pulled away from my mouth and his lips burned a trail down the curve my neck to my throat and finally across the top of one tit to my nipple. He teased it with his tongue until my knees weakened and I could only think about where else I'd like his mouth.

I pulled away and headed for the bedroom. Behind me I heard Dominic's sigh and the sloppy release of his cock by Stan's mouth. I'd untangled myself from my dress and bra by the time I reached the bed. Stan had pulled back the down comforter exposing bright red satin sheets. Dominic got to the bed at the same time I did and he knelt in front of me. He kissed his way down my belly and followed the silk of my stockings as he pulled them away from my hips and along the length of my legs. I fell back on the bed so he could pull off my boots, hose, and panties.

Dominic kissed the arch of my foot and then proceeded to drag his lips up my calf and along the inside of my thigh. I opened my legs to welcome him, but he licked his way back to my foot and then started up the other leg. By the time he pulled apart my lips with his long fingers, I was dripping all over the sheets. I planted my heels on the bed and pushed my hips toward his face. He laughed and blew hot breath on my pussy. That only made me wetter and I groaned in frustration.

Fortunately, he took the hint and dragged his talented tongue the length of my slit. He pressed the flat of his tongue on my clit and turned his head just slightly from side to side. I gasped. Out of the corner of my eye, I saw Stan crawl in from the bathroom and position himself on his knees beside the bed. I stuck out one foot and Stan licked my toes while Dominic diddled my clit with the point of his tongue and cupped my breasts in his large hands. I moaned and tangled my fingers in his hair, pulling him closer.

Stan sucked my toes into his mouth, Dominic squeezed my breasts, and wrapped his lips around my clit while still teasing it with the point of his tongue. I exploded in his face, screaming and shaking as the orgasm pushed every coherent thought from my mind. I heard Dominic chuckle and Stan tear open a condom package. I couldn't lift my head. Fortunately Dominic was intuitive enough to stand. I watched Stan roll the condom over Dominic's cock, knowing the man would get to put it where his was never allowed.

Dominic lifted my legs and turned me so that I lay properly on the bed. He stretched out next to me and caressed me from breast to outer thigh. My hips rose up, seeking his touch between my legs, but he ignored my still throbbing pussy. He kissed me, this time thrusting his tongue deep into my mouth sharing my own juices with me. I pulled on his arm and he moved on top of me, settling between my thighs. I was panting, my hips thrusting up to meet his. He slid inside me and I gasped. Then I pushed up to take more of him and felt him nudge my cervix.

We found our rhythm in the beat of the drums that still spilled out of the speakers hidden in the walls. Stan kissed whatever he could reach without interfering with Dominic, a finger, a toe, my shoulder. Without pulling out, Dominic rose to his knees, and pulled my legs across his thighs. Stan wasted no time and pushed his face between my legs. He alternated between tonguing my clit and licking my juices off Dominic's cock when it emerged from my pussy. Someone's hand squeezed my tit, and another had inserted itself between me and the sheets and was caressing my ass.

I could no longer move and let Dominic pull out and thrust back in while Stan licked away. My eyes rolled back in my head, every muscle in my body tensed, and I screamed again. I shuddered from my pussy outward and I vaguely remember hearing Dominic give a low grunt as he slammed inside me. Stan pulled away and Dominic settled on his side next to me, his head on my shoulder, one arm across my waist, and his now flaccid penis draped across my thigh still encased in latex. Stan removed the condom and wiped him clean with a damp washrag. I just floated in postorgasmic bliss.

"Wow," Dominic whispered in my ear. "I'm going to have to make sure I perform in this town more often."

I managed to open one eye. "You are welcome to perform here anytime you'd like."

Two Brothers

By I.G. Frederick

After dropping the kids off at their father's house for one of his weekend visitations, I stopped for paint and wallpaper. I planned to redecorate my children's rooms while they were gone, rather than repeat last month's fiasco. That weekend, instead of taking advantage of my freedom from soccer games and birthday parties to do needed repairs, I spent the entire time surfing the Internet. A visit to an erotica short story website proved barely titillating so I spent hours taking those free tours of porn sites (I couldn't bring myself to give up the personal information required to join). The weekend ended in a frenzied search for cookies and browser history files to erase, so my computer genius son wouldn't find out what his mother had been doing in his absence.

As usual, I parked my cherry-red convertible at the far end of the lot, hugging a landscape island, to avoid getting her dinged. Rita still looked as sharp as when I drove her off the lot the day after my divorce was final, four years ago. Holding the button that raised the ragtop and clicking the fastenings in place, I noticed two young men hanging out next to a battered pickup truck with the hood up. They gave us the once over as I climbed out. I knew they looked mostly at the car. I'm almost forty-five and, although I try to keep in shape, childbearing did take its toll and my hair already shows streaks of grey. Still, I could feel the young men's eyes turn from Rita and follow me through the parking lot. They probably wondered how an old mom got such a sharp ride. I swayed my hips provocatively to let them know that while not young, I'm not dead either. I wore tattered cut offs and an old t-shirt — great for painting, but hardly sexy. But, they were tight and showed off what I like to call a voluptuous figure.

I forgot about the boys while I shopped, and was surprised to see them when I pushed my cart — filled with paint, wallpaper, detergent, and other household necessities — back out to my car. The truck's hood had been lowered and they each rested a foot on the rear bumper. I gave Rita a quick once-over to make sure they hadn't taken their frustration out on my baby. When your husband of fifteen years leaves you for his twenty-two-year-old, size-two secretary, you take whatever consolation you can get — in my case a sporty, red, five-speed that guys drooled over. I opened the trunk and puzzled about how to squeeze in the cart's contents. Out of the corner of my eye, I saw the shorter of the two men nudge the taller until he ambled over and helped me stow my purchases. Better than six feet tall and all muscle, he wore tight, worn blue jeans, scuffed cowboy boots, and a red, checked cotton shirt that clung to his skin. He smelled of engine oil, sweat, and hay.

I slammed the trunk and turned to thank him. He looked down at me with his wide-brimmed cowboy hat in his hands, his face rugged and tanned as if he spent most of his working days outside.

"Excuse me, ma'am, can I ask you a very personal question?" He shifted his weight from one foot to the other. Maybe he'd never seen a cherry-red convertible driven by a 45-year-old divorcée.

I nodded, curious.

"You see, ma'am, my brother and me are from Lima, Montana, and we've never been to the big city before." Somehow I'd never thought of Boise, Idaho, as the big city. "Before he died, my pappy told us that the first time we got laid we should find a woman with some experience 'cause she would show us how to do it right. We're both still virgins, and we were wondering if you might be interested in teaching us."

My mouth dropped open. I fell against the trunk, but jumped back up when the sun-heated metal burned bare legs below my cutoffs. Well, I had to give him points for originality — I had never heard a pickup line like that.

His eyes stayed glued to the toes of his boots. "I know this is a little abrupt and I beg pardon, but we noticed you weren't wearing a wedding ring, and we thought maybe a woman who drove a car like that," he pointed his hat at Rita, "and walked the way you do might be," he cleared his throat, "might be more willing than most to consider breaking us in."

I just stared at him, working my eyes down his muscular chest to the crotch of his jeans. A decent size bulge, but he could have stuck socks in there. I don't know if pheromones, the fact that I hadn't had sex with a man in four years, or the heat, made me decide to play along, for the moment.

"Well, now, that would depend on what you had to offer." I kept my voice low and husky and ran one finger along his zipper. The bulge grew and his face turned bright red.

He cleared his throat again. "I believe, ma'am, that I may be a little bigger than normal, but I really have no way of knowing."

"What about your brother?"

"He's not as big as I am, ma'am."

I looked at the other young man, shorter and more wiry than his brother, watching us from under his hat. I thought about dated wallpaper and peeling paint as well as long lonely nights alone with a rubber dong — afraid to use a vibrator because the kids might hear it.

"I'd have to really see what you had to offer before I agreed to anything." I couldn't believe I said that.

He shifted his weight again and scanned the area. Cars were filling the lot. "If you came over to the truck, I could stand behind the door. You and Pete could block the view and I could ... give you a peek."

I envisioned the two of them throwing me in the pickup and taking me somewhere to rape me.

But then why ask? Intrigued, I walked with him over to the truck. Pete and I stood side by side next to the open driver's side door. The young man, he couldn't have been much more than 19, stood with his back to the truck's interior, pulled down his zipper and extracted the longest, thickest cock — even only half-erect — I have ever seen in real life. I reached out and ran my finger along the bottom. It stood at full attention — eight inches long and almost two inches thick. I decided I wanted to be the first woman to sit on it.

I looked up in the man's face and saw his eyes for the first time. A piercing blue, they stared right through me, as if he could see how much I needed a man's touch again.

"Where you boys staying?" I asked.

"We just got into town this morning, and haven't found a place yet." He stood there with his cock hanging out of his jeans. "We stopped here to get some oil for the truck."

I could see remnants of hay bales strewn about the pickup's bed; they'd probably slept in there for a couple of nights. I turned around toward the highway and heard the sound of a zipper closing behind me. "There's a halfway decent motel over by the interstate exit." I pointed in the general direction. You could see the sign from where we stood. "You boys go over there and get a room. I'll follow." I wasn't about to take these fellows home — I figured I risked enough going to a motel with them. Pete walked around and climbed into the passenger side. I looked up at his brother. "Do you have condoms?"

He shook his head.

"Well, go in the store and get some. I'll wait in my car."

"Uh, ma'am, how many should we get?"

I smiled. I should give these boys a lesson to remember. "At least a dozen, maybe two — 12 for each of you. And while you're there, get some lube."

His big grin revealed even teeth, white against his sun-darkened face. "Yes, ma'am!"

"My name is Audrey. Please don't call me ma'am any more."

"Yes, m... Audrey. I'm Paul." He extended his hand. "Pleased to make your acquaintance, Audrey."

I put my hand in his big, calloused palm, but instead of shaking, he lifted it to his lips and kissed my fingertips. I guess they watch old movies in Lima.

He and his brother loped into the store. They returned to the truck — with a very full plastic bag — less than ten minutes later. I started Rita's engine, lowered her top, put her in gear, and killed the motor with too much clutch. My sensible self screamed at me to scurry home, but as much as I feared trouble, I also couldn't remove the image of Paul's huge cock from my mind.

The boys waved to me, jumped into their truck, and headed back toward the interstate. I waited in the parking lot across from the motel while Paul went into the office. I'd completely lost my mind. Couple of barely legal kids, they probably would get off the minute I let them touch me. Despite my doubts, I followed the pickup to the back of the motel, found a safe parking spot in a corner, and raised Rita's top. I took a deep breath — last chance to back out — but climbed out of the car and walked toward the room.

The minute we stepped inside the room, Pete grabbed me, pawed my breasts, and planted sloppy kisses on my mouth. He reeked as if he hadn't bathed in several days. For a moment I panicked, then I pushed him away. He didn't resist and I relaxed a little.

"First lesson — never grab a woman. Lovemaking should be slow and gentle. Now, I want to know the truth. Are you boys really virgins?" They both blushed. I was charmed.

"Yes, m... Audrey," Paul stuttered. "Neither of us has ever been with a woman before."

I am going to enjoy this so much, I thought.

"Okay, I want you boys to each take a shower. And I want you to jack off while you're in there." They looked at me, eyes wide, mouths opened. I softened my voice. "If you've never been with a woman you're likely to come the minute you get inside me. Not much fun for me." They still stood there staring and shaking their heads. I slapped Paul on the rump. He jumped, but headed for the bathroom, closing the door behind him.

"Leave it open. I want to watch." He stared at me again, then pulled off his clothes.

I couldn't see an ounce of fat anywhere on his body, every muscle was defined under his sun-darkened skin. The tan stopped at his waist, but his legs looked as powerful as his chest and arms. His prick stuck straight out. I stepped into the bathroom and pulled the opaque shower curtain back a little.

When he was all soapy, Paul stroked his lovely cock while staring straight at my tits. I pulled the t-shirt over my head, dropping it on the floor, and unfastened my bra. He shot his load as soon as my double-D cups (hey, I've nursed two kids) fell out of the lace. Paul spurted across the shower and hit the opposite wall. He blushed again and turned his back so he could rinse off.

The minute Paul got out of the shower to towel dry, Pete stripped and stepped in. Not as well endowed as his brother, his dick was nothing to be ashamed of. Although wiry where his brother was thick, Pete looked just as strong. It didn't take him as long to jack off. His load didn't reach the wall either.

With both of them now clean and naked in the room, I hesitated. I was so wet, I could have taken either of them right then and there. But they wanted a teacher, and I wanted to make sure they didn't get by on their physical endowments — that they learned how to treat women right. I took Paul's hand and led him to one of the double beds. Pulling back the covers, I pushed him gently until he sat down on the sheets. I took his face in my hands, and leaned down to kiss him. I smiled inwardly; he tasted of breath mints.

I teased his tongue with mine, luring it into my mouth. Reaching down, I put his hands on my bottom. He massaged my ass for a few minutes then, slid his big hands up along my back and down across my shoulders to my breasts. While he fondled them, I moved my head so his mouth found its way down my neck. He had learned the first lesson well — his lips traveled very slowly along the sensitive skin, across my collarbone to my breasts. He moaned when he got my nipple in his mouth and I could see his cock rising again. I ran my fingers through his hair.

"Here, you need to pay attention to the woman you're with and adjust to her preference." I was panting, but they expected me to teach. "Some women like you to be rough with their tits, biting their nipples and sucking hard. Me, I prefer soft nibbles and licking." Paul wrapped his tongue around my nipple, making me groan. I unbuttoned my shorts and pushed them and my wet underpants to my hips.

Moving his mouth to my rounded belly, Paul pulled my clothing down around my ankles. I stepped out of them and lay on the bed, my legs dangling over the side. I pulled Paul's head down and pushed him toward my soaked pussy.

"You can never go wrong eating a woman's pussy boys. If she isn't ready, that will get her wet. If she's having second thoughts, they'll disappear. And, she's liable to return the favor."

I couldn't see Paul's face, but Pete, stood in the bathroom doorway, staring at us, eyes wide, mouth open, cock hard.

Paul buried his face in my pussy, licking on my clit until I bucked up against his face, an orgasm washing over my entire body. I wrapped my legs around his head, pressing my cunt against his mouth.

When the spasms stopped, I lay limp. My legs slid down Paul's shoulders. He lifted his head, his face dripping with my pussy juices, and looked quite pleased with himself. I tugged on his hair and he kissed his way back up my body, stopping for a while at my breasts but finally finding his way back to my mouth. I sucked my juices off his lips. His cock pressed against my thigh.

"Hand me one of those condoms, sweetie." Without releasing my lips, Paul grabbed the plastic bag, and although he spilled most of the contents on the floor, he eventually presented me with one foil packet. I pushed him back, ripped open the wrapping, and rolled the sheath down his magnificent shaft.

"When you first enter a woman, you want to take it slow — especially someone as big as you. You can use your hand to guide it inside her."

I put my feet on his shoulders, opening my thighs wide so Paul could see. He took his cock in his right hand and, with an adorably serious look, eased it into my wet cunt. He groaned and his expression changed to one of ecstasy. His eyes closed and he slid deep inside. I felt as if he was splitting me in two. I slid my legs down his chest, wrapped them around his back, and tightened my grip to keep him from moving. When I felt comfortable with all that meat, I dropped my feet to the bed and pushed against him. He took the hint and moved in and out. I almost wept from the intensity of the sensations bombarding me.

"Now, here again you should follow the woman's lead," I had a hard time keeping my voice steady. "Some women like it slow and easy like this. Others want you to slam it into them, hard. I'm one of those."

Paul didn't need any more explanation. He pulled his

hips back and rammed me with a force that shook the bed. He found a hard, steady rhythm. My tits bounced around, and his balls smacked against my rear. I cried out as the second orgasm took over, my entire body shaking. I opened my eyes just in time to watch the delight cross his face when my pussy clenched around his shaft. He thrust harder and my orgasm didn't stop until he spasmed.

When he started to pull away, I wrapped my legs around his back. "Never pull it out, hon, unless you come before she does. Then you need to get down there with hands or mouth right away and bring her off. But if you've done it right, you want to stay inside as long as you can."

Paul kissed me. His eyes widened again when he realized my pussy continued to spasm. "Are you still coming?"

"No, it's kind of like the aftershock of an earthquake. If the orgasm is intense enough, the pussy will keep twitching for quite a bit. One reason not to pull out too soon." I smiled up into intense blue eyes and deepened my voice. "That way you can enjoy it, too."

Paul grinned.

"What about me?" Pete's voice trembled. *Poor baby, watching big brother have all the fun.* As soon as Paul softened and slipped out, I pushed at his chest and he rose to his feet. I sat up and patted the bed and Pete didn't waste time accepting my invitation. He started to grab me again, but then hesitated, gently wrapped his arms around me, and kissed me. I wondered if Paul had as little experience as he claimed. Pete's kisses, unlike Paul's, were sloppy and clumsy. I pulled back. "More lip, less tongue, sweetie," I whispered, "and try to keep your saliva to yourself." I suspected everything had been staged to get little brother's cherry popped. Then I remembered the look on Paul's face when he felt my pussy wrapped around his cock — definitely his first time.

I put one of Pete's hands on my breast. He squeezed it gently — at least he paid attention — and leaned down to take the nipple in his mouth. He was breathing heavily and I wondered if the boy would last until he got inside me. I pushed him back on the bed, and sat on his face. Unlike his brother, Pete apparently, knew nothing about female anatomy.

I lifted myself off and looked down at his wet face. "Do you know what a clitoris is, honey?" He looked chagrined and shook his head. "It's the most sensitive part of a woman's body. Very few women can orgasm if you don't stimulate their clitorises in some way." I pulled my nether lips apart and showed him. Pete needed no more instruction. He dove right in, licking and sucking my nob until I shuddered and came all over his face.

I grabbed a condom off the night stand and slid down Pete's chest — leaving a trail of my juices in the thick mat of hair — until I felt his erect cock against my butt. Straddling his thighs while I sheathed him, I watched his face. He bit his lip, probably trying to avoid coming too soon. I figured I'd get a head start and grabbed his cock, rubbing it against my clit. His eyes rolled back in his head and he groaned. Without releasing him, I raised myself up and positioned the head of his dick between my cunt lips. I lowered myself, staring at his face. Pete's eyes opened wide and his lips parted, revealing perfect white teeth. I moved up and down his shaft, and he reached up to cup my breasts in his hands, teasing my nipples between his thumbs and forefingers. Bucking his hips he adjusted his rhythm until it matched my own. I rubbed my clit against him with the down stroke and lost control when the throbbing between my legs traveled the length of my body. Pete's hands slid down and grabbed my ass, moving me up and down as he thrust into me. He lasted longer than I expected and when he did come, he screamed so loudly I worried someone would complain to the management.

I collapsed on his chest and we lay there, panting, until he popped out. I rolled onto my back, and before I could think about what to show them next, Paul lay beside me, kissing me and playing with my tits. His hard cock pressed against my hip. Doing them one at a time created a problem, I decided. The other one got aroused again watching me with his brother. At this rate, exhaustion would kill me before lunch. Time to try out one of my all-time favorite fantasies.

"How'd you boys like to both fuck me at the same time?"

Two pairs of wide-open blue eyes stared at me. I pushed off the bed, threw a condom at each of them, and rummaged through the bag to find a large tube. While they tried to get the rubbers on, I slathered my fingers and lubed up my ass. I had Paul lay in the middle of the bed and smeared lube all over Pete's only semi-hard cock. How the hell he had managed to get the condom on, I didn't know. When he was hard and well-lubricated. I eased myself down onto Paul's gorgeous shaft and leaned forward on my hands, putting my ass in the air.

"Okay, Pete, put it in SLOWLY."

I sensed no movement behind me and finally Paul shouted. "In her ass dickhead, she wants you to fuck her in the ass." He lowered his voice. "You should have let me have the back end."

"Sorry sweetie, you're way too big for me to take that way."

Pete pulled my butt cheeks apart with his hand and pressed the head of his penis against my asshole. I relaxed and he slid it partially in, then hesitated. "You're doing fine, hon. Just ease it in nice and slow." I closed my eyes enjoying the sensation of being completely filled from both ends. Paul waited until Pete had sunk in all the way to his balls and then he moved up and down inside me. Pete eased himself almost all the way out and then pushed back in. I just held still, eyes closed, getting thoroughly fucked. Pete reached around and played with my tits. Paul massaged my clit with his thumb. I had to concentrate to keep my arms straight as wave after wave of orgasm pulsed through me. Just a mass of over stimulated nerves, I could no longer see — no longer hear myself screaming. I'm didn't even notice the boys getting off, but suddenly they both lay still and I could feel them softening inside me.

"This end you need to pull out of, Pete, just do it slowly, please." When he inched himself free from my now very sore asshole. I dropped, managing to land next to Paul's legs instead of on top of them. I pressed myself along Paul's side with my head on his shoulder and my arm across his chest. Pete plastered himself along my backside and let his hand rest on my waist. We panted and I drifted in a post orgasmic stupor, my pussy muscles throbbing incessantly.

By the time our breathing returned to normal, I could have fallen asleep, but I wanted an answer to the question that had been nagging at me all morning.

"Paul, how is it you seem so much more knowledgeable than Pete?"

"I had a buddy in high school whose dad worked for some high-tech firm in San Francisco. They had satellite Internet and when his dad travelled we would check out some," he cleared his throat and I could see a tinge of red creeping up from his neck, "very educational, adult sites."

I laughed. Paul's stomach rumbled, followed immediately by grumbling from Pete's belly. I looked at the clock — almost noon. I had Pete find the phone book and we called up the first Chinese restaurant listed that delivered. I wanted to make sure my boys kept up their strength. They still had lots more condoms and I had oh so many more positions to show them. And I couldn't wait to watch their faces when I gave them their first blow jobs

Honeymoon

By I. G Frederick

Lewis thought it best to keep the wedding small and save our money for the honeymoon since we both were marrying for the second time. At first, we couldn't agree on where to go. I had so many places on my hope-to-visit list. But Lew, who had traveled much more than I, insisted he wanted to spend the time enjoying me rather than exploring someplace I'd never seen. After much persuasion, I agreed to a Caribbean cruise. With all the last-minute details required for even a small wedding, I gratefully accepted Lew's offer to make the travel arrangements. His reluctance to share specifics perturbed me a little, though.

The wedding turned into a rather one-sided affair. My parents, two brothers, sister-in-law, and several of my friends joined us, and a judge, in the Forest Preserve. Lew's parents live in South Dakota and couldn't make it. His best friend, he told me, couldn't get back into the country on time. Apparently, Lew didn't invite anyone else. My older brother, Richard stood up as Lew's best man.

I tried to forget the nagging feeling that Lew didn't want his partners, friends, and family to know he had married a divorced forty-something waitress with a useless degree in art history who lived in the proletarian suburb of Wheeling, Illinois. Instead, I looked forward to our trip. Although I had sailed on Lake Michigan with Lew, I had never ventured out on anything bigger than the dinner boats with their skyline views. My friends chipped in to buy me proper cruise wear as a wedding present. They all thought marrying a high-powered Chicago attorney and moving to a big house in Northbrook sounded like a fairytale come true. But for me, I had to really think about getting married again -- unsure if I could love Lew enough to adjust to a lifestyle I'd never wanted.

We finally arrived on Tortola after a day -- that had started before dawn -- of crowded airports, cramped plane seats, and bad food. I really looked forward to some cruise ship pampering, but the taxi dropped us off at a marina in front of a sixty-five foot yacht.

I turned to Lew, ready to cry. "I thought we were going on a cruise? I bought fancy dresses and everything." I bit my lip and swallowed so I wouldn't sound petulant. "I'd hoped to enjoy a massage in the spa, or at least soak in a hot tub, after this wretched day we've had." I had read all about the amenities of cruising and had planned to experience every one of them. I wondered if Lew feared I would embarrass him by using the wrong fork or dressing inappropriately for dinner.

He pulled me into his arms, and ran his fingers through my hair until my head found its resting place on his shoulder. "We are going on a cruise, sweetheart. And we'll go out for dinner on some of the islands so you'll get to wear your fancy dresses." He gave my hair a little tug, forcing me to look up into his amazing blue eyes. Short curly black hair and a square chin gave Lew the look of a movie star. I always wondered what he saw in me with my unmanageable, mousy brown hair, brown eyes, ordinary nose, and ridiculous number of freckles. "And, I promise, you'll be so pampered for the next week, you won't ever want to go home."

I didn't believe him, but I swallowed my tears.

At that moment, a bronzed Adonis wearing nothing but a pair of cut-off shorts stepped off the boat and threw his arms around my husband. "Welcome to Tortola, Lew." Taller than Lew by several inches, the man had a muscular body and big, calloused hands. He wore his long blond hair pulled back in a ponytail, and his clean-shaven face had the rugged look of someone who spent most of his days outdoors.

When he released Lew, who had returned the embrace, I stuck out my hand. The Adonis took it in his and lifted it to his lips. "You must be Allison. Lew was right; you are lovely. I'm Seth, co-owner of the *Mallory Todd* and half your crew for the coming week."

I felt my face growing hot. I do try to take care of myself: I work out regularly and watch what I eat. But no one would call me lovely. The only flattering word for my figure is voluptuous, and that's being kind.

I turned to Lew, curious about the reception we'd received, but the two men gathered up the bags the taxi driver had scattered on the dock. I followed them across the gangplank into the pilot house. *Oh well*, I thought, *I guess I'll live without a hot tub, and maybe I can persuade Lew to give me a back rub.*

When we stepped aboard, a beautiful woman climbed up the steps from the galley and salon below. "Welcome aboard the *Mallory Todd*." Her eyes ran me up and down. "I see you've met Seth. I'm Joanna, cook, first mate, purser." She winked. "Whatever Seth can't do for you, I can."

At that moment, I seriously thought about turning around and finding a taxi to take me back to the airport. Joanna had everything I didn't: a firm rear end, taut belly, and perky breasts visible under her tight, pink t-shirt and skin-hugging white shorts. Her long blonde hair swept the middle of her back and her eyes sparkled like emeralds. I caught the lustful look she directed at my husband and I knew I couldn't win any competition with Aphrodite. I just hoped Seth kept

Joanna happy and she wasn't one of those women who went after any man, married or not, just for the challenge.

Joanna grabbed my hand in both of hers. "Glad to meet you Allison, I am so looking forward to getting to know you better this week."

I stared at her, wondering just what kind of conversations my husband had had with the crew of the *Mallory Todd*, just how long he had known Seth, and why a beautiful woman like Joanna would want to know more about me.

"I know you two must be exhausted after traveling all day. Seth, will you take their bags to their cabin? If you like, Allison, you have time to unpack and take a bath, before dinner."

A bath? Who ever heard of a bathtub on a sailboat?

We followed Seth past the galley into the forward cabin and I watched while he piled our five suitcases on the settees on either side. Three steps led from the entry to a king-size berth that filled one corner. A cast iron stove, painted in French blue and creamy white enamel, sat on a tile hearth between one settee and the large, black walnut desk that occupied the corner opposite the berth.

Lew lifted one of my suitcases onto the bed. "Why don't you just unpack what you think you'll need for a few days while I fill the tub. I'll have Seth stow the suitcases where he can get them for us if you find you're missing something later."

I looked at Lew, but he didn't appear to be joking. He stepped outside the cabin and opened a door to the right. A moment later, I heard water running. I pulled out underwear, bathing suits, shorts, t-shirts, and sunscreen and found room for them in drawers under the bed and the settees. I left the fancy coverups and the other cruise wear and most of the dresses in the suitcase, although I did hang my two nicest ones in the tiny armoire built under the raised berth.

Lew had the tub three-quarters full when I stepped around the corner to join him. Steam drifted over the top of the water and condensed on the mirror above the porcelain sink. The round Japanese tub looked big enough for two. A slatted wooden lounge sat next to it along the bulkhead.

"Go ahead and soak for a bit while I unpack. I'll come wash your back in a few minutes." Lew kissed the side of my neck.

Lew closed the door behind him and I stripped off my blouse, jeans, bra and cotton briefs and hung them on the back of the door. I climbed onto the lounge and dipped my legs into the hot water, getting used to the temperature before I eased myself over the side and into the tub. Lew apparently made quick work of his own unpacking, because I had only relaxed for a short while when he returned. I leaned back against the side of the tub, eyes half closed, and watched him undress through my lashes. I admired the hard lines of his chest, the bulge of his arm, the muscular curve of his legs. I never understood what interested Lew in me -- I didn't have looks or money or even a career and I was seven years older than he -- but, then, I avoided asking.

Lew swung one leg over the side of the tub and then the other and settled into the water beside me. "Now, I believe I promised to wash your back." He kissed the tip of my nose and reached for the bar of soap next to a yellow rubber duck that sat between the taps. Tossing aside the paper wrapping, he rubbed soap all over my back, his hands sliding around my sides to caress my breasts with slippery softness. He cupped both of them in his hands and kissed the side of my neck. I leaned back into his caress, but the trill of a brassy bell interrupted us.

Seth's voice boomed: "Dinner."

"I'm not really hungry." I turned in Lew's embrace and lifted my face toward his.

"We can't be rude, darling. We'll have plenty of time," he nibbled on my ear, "later."

I wanted to ask him why the crew should dictate our schedule. We were on our honeymoon, surely they would understand if we wanted time alone together. But Lew had already pulled the plug and the water gurgled down the drain. I rinsed the soap off my back and breasts with the shower hose and let Lew help me climb out of the tub. We dried off, dressed and found our way to the salon next to the galley. The bath had taken what was left of my energy and I almost fell asleep at the table. Lew helped me back to our cabin and took off my clothes, but I fell asleep before he got into bed.

When I woke, sunlight poured in through the portholes that lined the aft bulkhead. I could feel the movement of the boat -- not the gentle rocking I remembered from the night before, but an up and down motion that told me we'd set sail. My stomach roiled and I tried to crawl over Lew to get to the head. Lew embraced me, running his hands up and down my back, pausing to squeeze my rear. But when he opened his eyes, he must have recognized the green look on my face. He helped me get out of bed, pull on a robe, and stumble into the head.

I was rinsing out my mouth when he knocked on the door. He handed me a swimsuit and t-shirt. "You should get dressed. I promise, once we get you up on deck, you'll feel much better."

Great, I thought. I'm stuck on a small boat with the Love Goddess and I'm too ill to have sex with my husband. I'd never experienced seasickness when we sailed on Lake Michigan, but then I spent all my time up on deck.

I struggled into the suit, a one-piece with tummy control that didn't really and a skirt to hide my thunder thighs, pulled the oversized t-shirt on over it, and opened the door to find Lew, sunscreen in hand, wearing only a small bikini. He took my hand and led me through the short narrow passageway to the stairs leading from the galley to the pilot house then out onto the deck. He lifted me up so I could sit on the roof of the salon.

"Good morning, you two," Joanna appeared with a glass of pineapple juice in each hand. "Any requests for breakfast?"

"I'm not hungry, thanks." I muttered.

Joanna looked me over. "Seasick?"

I nodded.

"No problem, we'll keep you up on deck while we're under

sail. Just remember to look at the horizon and you'll be fine."

She turned to Lew and I imagined her appreciating his barely-there bikini. "From now on we'll make sure you two are up before we weigh anchor in the morning. And we only sail once at night so you can sleep in the cabin most of the time. We can rig a bed for the two of you up here, or you can sleep on the bunks in the pilot house, on the night we don't anchor. Here," she handed me one of the glasses, "this should help."

I found that being up in the fresh air and looking out to the horizon settled my stomach. The thought of breakfast no longer made me queasy.

Seth laid deck pads for us between the windows of the pilot house and the hatch that ventilated the salon. I felt self-conscious -- he and Joanna could watch us over the wooden wheel when they took turns at the helm -- so I kept my t-shirt on. I rubbed sunscreen on my arms, face, and legs and handed the bottle to Lew. He gave me a strange look, then sighed and smeared lotion on his face, arms, chest, and legs. He looked at the bottle, looked at me, and looked at the bottle again. At that moment, Joanna appeared, carrying a tray laden with fruit, muffins, and a pot of coffee. The smell of hot cinnamon and nuts drifted up from the muffins to compete with the aroma of the coffee. She set the tray down and took the bottle from Lew.

"Here you two, dig in. I'll put some of this lotion on your back, Lew."

I raised one eyebrow at her eagerness to touch my husband, and wondered why Lew hadn't asked me to put sunscreen on his back.

"Thanks, Joanna."

I guess I shouldn't have expected him to turn down her offer, but I resented the fact that he didn't.

Lew poured a cup of coffee, stirred in sweetener and cream and handed it to me. "Maybe you can talk Allison out of her t-shirt, too." Lew filled another cup, blew at the hot liquid, and then took a sip. "Fabulous coffee and these muffins smell wonderful."

Lew offered one to me, but I shook my head and reached for a slice of mango instead. I couldn't exactly pig out on muffins while Aphrodite smeared lotion on my husband's back -- and he enjoyed it.

"You should take off your shirt, Allison," Joanna said. "In fact, you can both take off your suits and get an all-over tan, if you like. We can warn you before we encounter another boat and you'll have plenty of time to cover up."

I almost dropped my cup. I had a hard enough time letting Lew see me naked. I certainly had no intention of parading around with everything jiggling for comparison with Miss Hard Body.

"No, thanks," I said to Joanna's receding back. I swallowed half of what was left in my cup, set it down on the tray, and flopped onto my belly.

Lew shrugged, and sat watching me while he ate. "I'm sorry this isn't what you expected, Allison. I just don't like those big, floating hotels. And, I thought you'd enjoy being away from the crowds." He brushed muffin crumbs off his hands and stretched out on his side next to me. One hand drifted up my thigh and wiggled under my swimsuit to cup my ass.

I turned over on my side, putting a little distance between us.

"They can see us." I tilted my head in the direction of the pilot house. The glass reflected the light from the morning sun so I didn't know if Seth or Joanna sat there.

"So?" Lew slid closer and wrapped his arms around me, pulling me against his chest. "We're newlyweds, let's act like it." He covered my mouth with his and his tongue found its way between my lips.

I pressed against his shoulders with my hands; I wished we could go back to the cabin, but knew that would make me seasick. I certainly did not want to get carried away in front of our crew. Before I knew it, though, my arms wound around Lew's neck, I kissed him back, and my breathing got heavier. His strong hands drifted up under my t-shirt, sliding up and down my back, pulling me tight against his chest.

He brought one thigh up between mine, and pressed against the heat he had generated there. I realized what he wanted to do and tried to pull away, but I couldn't wriggle free of his embrace. I could hear his chuckle rumbling deep in his chest.

Lew had made a pass at me after he'd eaten lunch every day for a month where I worked at Bob Chinn's Crabhouse. I figured he offered my one and only chance to get laid by someone so incredibly good looking, and grabbed the opportunity. I've always enjoyed sex, but I had never experienced anyone as amazing as Lew. The next day, my fellow servers chastised me for not playing hard to get, but I didn't care. If I never had sex again in my entire life, I'd have no regrets. But, Lew kept coming back for more. Within a few weeks, we saw each other almost every night. For some reason, he got a real charge out of his ability to make me come just with kissing and touching. When we have sex, I just come over and over and over again. He claims a record of twenty-three times. I guess I believe him; I can never keep count.

We started spending entire days together -- sailing on the thirty-two-foot boat he co-owned with three other guys; listening to concerts in Grant Park; behaving like a couple of kids riding roller coasters at Six Flags; taking in the special exhibits at the art and history museums. We talked all the time about everything imaginable. Three months after our first date, Lew asked me to move in with him.

Now plastered against him, the crotch of my swimsuit getting wetter by the minute, I imagined Aphrodite or Adonis watching us, from the pilot house. But Lew kept up the pressure until I stopped caring. I rode his thigh to orgasm, almost swallowing his tongue to keep from crying out. Lew just grinned at me, like he always does, and I got lost in the cobalt blue of his eyes. I didn't even fight him when he lifted my arms and slipped the t-shirt over my head. I basked in the warm sun while he smeared sunscreen all over my exposed back. He slipped the straps off my shoulders. "I know one of those dresses you bought has a very low neckline." Lew planted a kiss on my shoulder. "Wouldn't want to spoil how it looks with tan lines."

Soon, with the rhythm of the boat bobbing up and down as it cut through the waves, the breeze caressing my skin on its way to fill the sail, and the warm sun beating down on my back, I drifted off to sleep. I woke up when Joanna brought us sandwiches, chips, and more fruit for lunch and worried about why she was always pushing food at me. Don't I already make her look svelte? Why does she want me to put on even more weight? I picked at half a sandwich and indulged in several pieces of juicy sweet mango and pineapple.

"You know," Joanna said when she came to take the tray, "eating lots of tropical fruit gives your skin a divine taste." She popped a piece of pineapple in her mouth and ran her tongue seductively across her lips. Although she looked at me while she did it, I knew she intended her little demonstration for Lew.

"Really?" I reached for the last slice of mango. "Then, I guess I'll just have to eat more."

"Oh, I'm sure you already taste heavenly."

Joanna picked up the tray and disappeared back around the pilot house, leaving me blinking in the sun, and the top of my suit sliding down to expose my nipples. I grabbed the fabric to pull it back over my breasts, but Lew stopped my hands.

"Don't, please. I think you would look delicious with an all-over tan." He reached down and licked first one nipple and then the other. Of course, they sprang to attention. Lew found the sunscreen bottle, poured lotion into his hands, and rubbed it onto my breasts and shoulders, pushing me down so I lay on my back on the deck pad. I tried to grab my suit, but he pulled it off of me, spreading sunscreen across my pasty white, and very round, belly. When he finished that, his fingers moved down and slipped in between my nether lips. I grabbed the sides of the deck pad to keep from bucking against him. He laughed, leaned down, and parted my bush. My eyes rolled back in my head.

Shortly after we started sleeping together. Lew had asked me to shave off my pubic hair. He promised it would make me more sensitive -- like I needed that. Now, with the sun beating down on my never-seen-sun pubes, I was glad I had resisted. His tongue found my clit and drove away my concerns about the sun and the audience in the pilot house until I came again. Lew just smiled and rubbed sunscreen on my thighs. I lay naked, all my flab exposed to the hard bodies surrounding me. I watched Lew slip out of his suit and flop down on his belly. I reached for the bottle and slathered lotion on his gorgeous, tight ass. I wanted to reach between his legs, but at that moment Joanna reappeared with the tray, this time bearing a pitcher of juice and empty glasses. I grabbed for my t-shirt, but Lew tossed it out of reach.

"I thought you might like to try my special papaya-mango-pineapple blend." She set the tray down in front of us and her eyes roamed over Lew's muscular body and my lumpy one. "Besides, you need to drink lots of fluids if you stay out in the sun all day."

I think I fell asleep again, because I heard the splash of the anchor in the water, saw Seth playing out the line from the bow, and realized the sun had neared the horizon. We apparently had lain in the shade of the pilot house for several hours, but the heat in the air kept us warm. The boat bobbed in front of a tiny spit of sand, no bigger than a grocery store. Only a couple of palm trees broke up the island's flat surface. I couldn't see another boat in our vicinity; I occasionally glimpsed a bit of white off in the distance, but no sails came into view.

"Perhaps you'd like a massage before dinner?" Joanna asked.

I rolled over on my stomach and looked at Aphrodite in her tight white shorts and powder blue t-shirt.

"We can pamper you just as well as any cruise ship staff. Both Seth and I have licenses."

I stared at her, my eyes opened so wide, my eyebrows almost reached my hairline. If I weren't married, and he weren't married, I would dearly love to get a massage from Seth. But he didn't make the offer, Joanna did.

"Sure, why not." As long as you don't try to give my husband a massage, I thought.

"I'll be right back." Joanna disappeared into the pilot house and emerged in moments with a bottle of massage oil. She poured oil into her hands and rubbed them together, warming it before she spread it on my back. The scent of coconut wafted up while her strong fingers rubbed the oil into my skin. I realized more hands worked oil into my feet. I tried to get up, but Joanna pressed me into the deck pad. If I turned my head one way, I could see Lew massaging my left foot. Turning my head to the other side, I stared at Seth rubbing away at the right. I considered protesting, but they made me feel so very good.

The three of them worked their way toward my waist, Joanna massaging first my neck and shoulders, then my arms and back. Seth and Lew started with my feet and rubbed their way up my legs until one of them straddled my thighs and massaged my buttocks. I realized that Seth's hands rubbed my backside when Lew kneeled in front of me and kissed me. "You won't get pampering like this on any cruise ship."

They turned me over onto my back and I had relaxed so much, I didn't even try to hide my belly. I lay sprawled on the deck pad, surrounded by naked gods and a goddess, sure I had found heaven. Seth and Lew rubbed oil on my breasts and then leaned down to take my nipples in their mouths. Joanna pushed my legs apart, kissed the inside of my thighs and then buried her face in my pussy. I gasped, and I came. Joanna giggled and the vibrations from the sound sent my pussy into new spasms. Lew chuckled and Seth just moaned around my nipple.

Hands roamed all over my body. I lifted my hips, pushing my pelvis into Joanna's face. My toes curled, and my ass muscles contracted while the tension built and I exploded over and over again.

Seth stretched out on the deck pad next to me, reached out, and rolled me on top of him, holding my hips while he slipped inside me. I tried to move, but he tightened his grip and kept me pressed against his pelvis. An oiled finger rimmed my asshole and pushed inside. First one, then two fingers oiled me inside and out. Finally, Lew's cock eased into my ass and I came as soon as the two men started moving. Propped up on my hands and knees, I just concentrated on enjoying the waves of pleasure coursing through me. Lew had promised me he would make all my fantasies come true and this was my number one.

Joanna positioned herself with a foot on either side of Seth's face. She had stripped off her shorts and shirt, and she tilted her shaved crotch at me. A ring with a red bead on it pierced her hood. I stuck out my tongue and discovered that she did taste sweet and fruity. I had never been with a woman, although I had confessed my curiosity to Lew. I knew what felt good to me, so I eagerly licked and kissed her until she moaned with delight. I discovered if I wiggled her ring with my tongue, Joanna groaned and writhed.

I'm sure I set a new record that evening, although Lew claims that for once even he lost count. I brought Joanna to orgasm several times before Seth and then Lew cried out and came one right after the other. I managed to collapse next to Seth instead of on top of him and Lew stretched out next to me, one hand draped over my waist.

Joanna and Seth jumped up. "You two relax while we go fix dinner." Joanna winked. "Tomorrow night, we'll give Lew a massage." Seth whispered something in Lew's ear and disappeared with Joanna.

I couldn't move. My pussy throbbed. Joanna's juices covered my face. "How much of this did you plan before we flew down here?" I asked Lew.

"Actually, Seth and I have known each other since college, he's the best friend who couldn't make it back into the country. They got another charter that ended the day before the wedding." Lew cleared his throat. "Seth and I have always shared our women. But the two of them had moved down here before you and I met, so we never got the chance to get together before now."

I turned over to face him and propped myself up on one elbow. "You always shared?" I wanted to shout at him, but I could hear Seth and Joanna clattering about in the galley below us and didn't want them to hear us argue.

"Well, it seemed like we never both had a girlfriend at the same time. Rather than leave the other guy out, we would do things together as a threesome, you know, go to movies or concerts, out to dinner."

I just stared at him, eyes wide. His face looked a little flushed, but I suppose that could have been sunburn.

"It didn't seem right that one of us would get to go home and get laid, so we started going home together, too."

"So you've been with Joanna before?" My voice sounded icy even to me, but I could only think about him pushing me to shave my pubic hair and wonder if he got the idea from her.

"Only as a threesome," he said as if that made it okay. "We thought it best if the odd man out never soloed with the other's lady."

I shook my head. "Why didn't you ever tell me about this?"

"About what? I never asked you about the relationships you had before we got together; didn't think I needed to provide references to verify my virility." Lew dragged one hand from my knee, across my hip, to the side of my breast.

I scowled. "You know that's not what I meant. I haven't planned any sexual encounters involving you and men I had relationships with in the past."

Lew's ran his finger along the side of my breast and teased my nipple. "Didn't you enjoy it?" He pouted.

I ignored his question and tried not to notice the way the touch of his finger on my nipple sent a thrill from my breast to my clit.

"When you and I started seeing each other, Seth and

Joanna were so excited about all of us getting together," Lew whispered. "But then you told me about your fantasy of making love with two men at the same time, so I decided to surprise you." I had confessed that to Lew when he told me he fantasized about eating naked pussy. I thought if he knew about a desire I had that would never happen, he wouldn't get upset when I decided not to try shaving.

Lew leaned over and sucked on my nipple until my breath came in ragged gasps. "Please tell me you're not mad at me," he mumbled into my breast.

I frowned and he looked like a lost puppy. Then, I decided I'd never have a better opportunity to finally ask the question that had haunted me since our first date. "Why in the world are you even interested in someone like me, Lew?"

"Whatever do you mean?" Lew pulled his lips away and stared at me.

I looked down at my breasts sagging to one side and my tummy protruding between us.

Lew cupped my chin in his hand. "Allison, you're the sexiest woman I have ever been with. I've never known a woman who enjoys sex as much or comes more often than you. Even Seth just admitted that he's a little jealous."

I just stared at him, incredulous. Seth, who married Aphrodite herself, jealous of my husband -- I couldn't wrap my mind around that notion.

Lew rolled me over on my back and pushed my legs apart with his knees. "How 'bout a little one-on-one for a change, my beautiful wife?"

I just crossed my ankles behind his back, unable to stay angry with a man who had made love to Joanna and still called me the sexiest woman he had known. I decided to stop worrying about how I looked and what conversations about me had taken place while my husband planned our trip. I would just enjoy my honeymoon and the pampering offered by my three gorgeous shipmates. After all, how could I argue who or what was attractive with the goddess of love and her consort?

Jail Bait
By I. G Frederick

After seeing him almost for six months, Serena decided Joshua was the man she wanted to take her cherry. But unlike every high school boy she'd ever dated, he didn't feel her up every chance he got, or insinuate that her lack of interest in having sex the third time they went out meant she was frigid. Even when she confided her most perverted fantasies, even after she told him she'd started taking birth control pills, he only kissed her on the cheek and said, "You're still jail bait, Babe."

Tomorrow her parents planned a huge family gathering at Devil's Lake in honor of her eighteenth birthday. But Joshua promised her that tonight would be even more special. She smoothed down the elegant little black dress that Joshua had bought her as an early birthday present. It fit like a glove, showing off her slender figure and revealing lots of cleavage and leg. Leaving the ladies room, she found him waiting in a corner booth overlooking the bay.

He stood up when she approached, ruggedly handsome

with straight chestnut hair and a muscular chest visible under his black polo shirt. She slid in so she sat between him and the wall.

"I've ordered you a virgin Piña Colada." He picked up the menu, but was interrupted almost immediately by the waiter setting drinks in front of them.

Serena sipped at the delightful combination of pineapple and coconut. She would never have known to ask for such a concoction. Dating an older man had so very many side benefits.

The waiter had returned without his tray and stood in front of their table, his hands behind his back. Joshua ordered the duck in lemon sauce. They both turned to her and the waiter said, "And for your daughter, sir?"

Joshua raised one eyebrow above the other. "She's not my daughter."

"Beg pardon, Sir." The waiter's facial expression didn't change. "What would you like for dinner, Miss?"

Serena was a bit taken aback by the prices, but since Joshua didn't seem to mind, she ordered the scallops in beurre blanc sauce. When the waiter left, Joshua lifted his martini glass and she clinked it with hers. He scooted closer and kissed the back of her neck. She melted against his shoulder. "You look beautiful in that dress. Thanks for forgoing undies," he whispered in her ear.

She blushed and buried her face against his neck.

"Our little secret." He took a sip of his drink from his right hand while his left drifted across her bare shoulders and pulled her closer. He toyed with her long, reddish brown hair, wrapping strands around his fingers then letting them pull free..

The heat between Serena's legs spread up to her chest, meeting the blush that had crept from her face to her neck. By the time the waiter set plates in front of them, the only thing she wanted to put in her mouth was Joshua's cock. She knew better than to suggest it, though. Dating horny high school boys who rarely took no for an answer, she'd gotten rather good at blow jobs. But Joshua always turned down her offers to demonstrate her skills on him. Since she couldn't have the meat she wanted, she settled for the delectable scallops with couscous. Joshua stole one of her scallops and shared tastes of his lemony duck with her.

Despite her protests that she was stuffed, Joshua insisted they share a berry cobbler with ice cream for dessert. By the time it arrived, they were the only patrons still in the restaurant. Staff had cleared and reset all the tables and she could hear a vacuum cleaner operating on the other side of the wall. She enjoyed the smooth creamy vanilla combined with tart berries and flaky crust. But she left most of the treat for Joshua.

When they emerged from the restaurant, the full moon had risen high in the sky and summer's heat had disappeared with the sun. Serena shivered and Joshua removed his blazer, wrapping it around her. With one arm across her shoulders, he led her away from the almost-empty parking lot and toward the bay.

They wandered along the spit and Serena could see the light of a bonfire burning near the cliff below the highway. When they reached it, she saw that two large driftwood logs had been pulled up to the cliff to provide a triangular shelter from the ocean breeze. A large blanket covered the sand between the fire and one log and a cooler sat between two camp chairs on the opposite side. Joshua glanced at his watch and guided Serena over to the chairs. "Thirsty?" He pointed at the cooler and sat down.

She shook her head.

"Cold?"

"Not now." She smiled and held her hands out toward the fire.

Joshua picked up a large gray Thermos® bottle from the sand next to the cooler. "Hot chocolate?"

She shrugged. "Sure, why not." Although the fire and his

jacket kept the chill away, Serena admitted to herself that she still wasn't exactly warm.

Steam drifted up from the plastic cups as Joshua filled them, handing one to her and putting the stopper back on the bottle before taking a sip from his. Serena held her cup with both hands, soaking in the warmth, and blew across the top, inhaling the rich aroma. The blanket indicated Joshua had more in mind than sharing cocoa, but he certainly didn't act like it.

The crackle of the fire and the lapping of waves on the sand punctuated the silence which neither seemed interested in breaking. Joshua kept looking at his watch while they sipped their drinks. Finally he grinned, his white teeth glistening in the firelight. He set his cup on the cooler, knelt in front of her, and ran his hands up her calves, until they reached her skirt which he edged above her knees. "It's midnight. Happy birthday, Babe." He kissed the insides of first one thigh and then the other just below her skirt. Serena gasped.

"Are you ready to become a woman tonight?"

She nodded enthusiastically. Finally.

Joshua rose up and kissed her, one hand behind her neck, the other sliding under her skirt. Their tongues twisted together in a cocoa-laced dance. His lips left hers and crept along her jaw to her throat, down her neck, until he buried his face in the cleavage exposed by the low-cut dress. Serena was panting and pushed off the jacket that had suddenly become too warm. He eased the straps of her dress down her shoulders, exposing her bare breasts to the chill air. With his tongue, he caressed her nipples until her hips involuntarily lifted off the chair. The heat between her legs had rushed above the temperature of the bonfire and she felt as if she was melting down there.

Leaving her nipples moist and erect, Joshua moved his mouth down to her legs again. He pulled gently, until her hips balanced on the edge of the chair. Pushing her skirt up as far as it would go, he kissed his way toward her hot, moist pussy. Holding her lips open with his fingers, he stuck out his tongue and slowly ran it from the bottom of her slit to her clit. A squeak escaped Serena's mouth and she heard it as if it had come from someone else. Joshua licked again and Serena slid further down in the chair, her knees finding their way up his arms to rest on his shoulders.

Each time his tongue caressed her virgin puss, the sensation became more intense. Her breathing became labored and she gripped the chair arms. Then he captured her clit with his lips and Serena exploded, her whole body shaking. She could feel herself gushing all over his face and worried that he would get upset with her.

"Such sweet honey," he muttered without emerging from between her legs. He licked and sucked until she shook again, crying out his name.

Joshua rose up, pulling her face toward his with one hand behind her neck. Serena hesitated, but let him press his lips to hers. Not a bad taste, actually, she thought with relief. No wonder he'd called it honey.

He stood up, pulled her to her feet, then lifted her in his arms. "Kick off your sandals." When she did, he wiped the sand off her feet with his handkerchief before setting her on the blanket. Then he removed his shoes, one at a time, stripping off his socks and placing his bare feet carefully on the blanket. "Don't want to roll around in sand." He looked at her from her naked breasts to her exposed bush with the dress still around her waist. "My God, you're beautiful." He held out his hands. "I've waited so long for this."

Stepping close to her, he pulled the dress over her head and dropped it on the blanket. Serena fell to her knees and fumbled with his belt, her hands shaking with anticipation, until she unbuckled it. While she got his dockers unzipped, he stripped off his shirt. She pulled down his slacks and he stood naked before her, the biggest cock she had ever seen pointing straight at her face. Serena stared at it, her eyes wide. The boys she'd sucked had miniature peckers compared to his and she panicked at the thought of taking him inside her virgin twat.

"Don't worry, Babe. I'll be gentle," he said, as if he could read her mind.

Serena took a deep breath and wrapped her lips around the head. He tasted so good and he wasn't the only one who had waited eagerly for tonight. She slid her lips as far as they would go which was only about half way down his cock. Wrapping her hand around the rest of his shaft, Serena slid her mouth back and forth. She discovered if she relaxed her throat to let him all the way in, she could get far enough for his pubic hair to tickle her nose. She breathed through her nose to avoid gagging. Joshua ran his fingers through her hair, but didn't push her head into his crotch or try to face fuck her.

Her jaw cramped up, so Serena rubbed his cock against her cheeks and pushed her tits up against either side of it. When she took him back in her mouth, she could tell he was close. She fisted the base of his cock with one hand, fondled his balls with the other, and sucked on his glans for all she was worth until he shot loads of hot, sweet cum into her mouth. She gulped it all down and then licked him from pubes to tip to make sure she hadn't missed any.

He dropped onto his knees besides her. "You weren't bragging, you really are good." He kissed her, wrapping his arms around her, pressing her breasts against his heated skin. Joshua pulled her down onto the blanket, laying next to her, his arms and legs wrapped around her, kissing her lips, her neck, her earlobes, stroking her hips, her ass, her breasts with his fingers. The distant roar of the ocean joined the sound of her heart and Jack's pounding in her ears.

Easing her onto her back, he gently pushed her legs apart and lay between them. He held his cock, hard again, in one hand and opened her lips with the other. Serena gasped as the tip entered her, pressing against her hymen. Joshua put one hand on either side of her face and looked into her eyes, the flicker of the firelight reflected in his irises. "Ready?"

She nodded and he pressed his lips hard against her, thrust his tongue deep into her mouth, and pushed himself into her. The sharp pain lasted only for a moment and she pushed her hips up into him. He pulled back and thrust again. With her mouth and cunt full of him, the tension started building in her clit again. She wiggled in delight and Joshua chuckled, pressing himself closer to her, gripping her ass cheeks. Serena tightened her arms around his back, holding on as she exploded yet again.

When she finally stopped trembling, Joshua rolled off of her. To her chagrin, she noted that the camp chairs had moved to the blanket side of the fire and that they were now both occupied with naked men. Serena blushed.

Joshua rose up onto his knees. "Babe, I want you to meet a couple of my frat brothers."

She pushed herself into a sitting position, cross-legged on the blanket with one hand holding each breast.

"This is Robert, we only call him Bob if we want to piss him off."

The man on her right stood, put one hand in front and one hand behind his waist and bowed. "Very pleased to make your acquaintance, Miss." He dropped to his knees and held one hand out to her. He had silky blond hair that brushed his shoulders and a pencil thin mustache. In the firelight, she could see a few strands of blond hair scattered across his chest and a v-shaped forest of them surrounding his very erect penis. Keeping one arm across her nipples, Serena lifted her right hand in his direction. He raised it to his lips and kissed each of her fingers in turn.

"And, this is Sid." Serena tore her eyes away from Robert to look at the naked man with curly read hair both on his head and at the cleft of his legs.

Although neither man was as big as Joshua, they both made her former boyfriends look inadequate. I'll never date a high school boy again, Serena promised herself.

Sid held out his hand until Serena reluctantly let go of her breasts and allowed him to kiss her fingers as well.

Joshua had maneuvered behind her. He cupped her perky tits in his large hands and kissed the back of her neck. "Robert and Sid are here to help me make your, as you call it, most perverted fantasy come true."

Serena's eyes opened wider and her gaze drifted from one to the other. Both grinned at her.

"Would you like that?" Jack's hot breath tickled her skin. She nodded. "Oh, yes, please."

Joshua chuckled again and nodded to Sid. He stretched out on his back near them and Joshua guided Serena into place, straddling his hips. Sid held his cock for her so she could sit on it.. When it slid inside her, he gasped and smiled at her.

Joshua had her lean forward on her hands. Sid caressed her tits and she felt a cold finger pressed against her butt hole. "Relax, Babe."

Serena took a deep breath as Joshua eased first one then two lube-slicked fingers up inside her. He withdrew and she felt him push his cock against her virgin ass. Sid waited until Joshua had eased himself inside her then with one hand on each of her hips, moved his own cock in and out of her puss. Serena moaned, balancing on her hands and knees, delighting in the sensation of having both her holes completely and utterly filled.

A hand stroked her hair and Serena looked up to see Robert's cock pointing at her mouth. She smiled, Joshua had gotten every detail of her fantasy exactly right. She opened her mouth just wide enough for Robert to slide it in. She was able to relax enough to get most of him down her throat without the aid of her hands.

The three men moved in unison, pounding into her with the rhythm of the waves hitting the sand. Joshua cupped her breasts in his hands, Robert played with her hair while he fucked her mouth, and Sid rubbed her clit with his thumb as he pushed up into her. Their breath came in short, quick gasps. Serena lost track of time and only the constant hammering of the surf kept her aware of where she was. Every inch of her body throbbed with pleasure even as she ached from over stimulation.

Every man's touch radiated through her body, settling in her clit. Sid's thumb pushed the intensity of the sensations to their peak. The shaking started in her toes and weakened her knees and elbows until she collapsed on top of Sid. The men kept moving in and out of her while she screamed, the sound muffled by Robert's cock filling her mouth and lost in the ocean's roar.

Robert came first, pulling out and spraying sticky cum all over her face. She licked her lips. He wasn't as sweet as Joshua, but she still enjoyed the taste. After a few more strokes, Sid and Joshua grunted and shot their load at the same time, sandwiching her between them while she trembled and twitched.

They held her until she could blink again. Sid had shrunk out of her by then. Joshua, eased himself out of her ass and stretched out next to her. She rolled off of Sid to lie between them and the two pressed up against her. Robert, sitting perpendicular to them all, pillowed her head on his thigh. Serena's cunt still throbbed, but the rest of her had stopped spasming.

Joshua started and the other two joined in singing, ever so softly: "Happy birthday to you, happy birthday to you, happy birthday beautiful Serena, happy birthday to you."

Nikki's Birthday

By I. G Frederick

I love Mistress very much, but I really miss having a man in my life. Yesterday, for my twenty-eighth birthday, she gave me a most wonderful present. I had asked to go to a local pizza place that has an indoor mini-golf course -- a chance to forget my age and indulge in juvenile pursuits. Mistress, who is quite a bit older, took me, but made it clear she would not play golf. When she went to purchase a round of golf, she asked me with whom I would play.

I shrugged. "I know you're not interested, I guess I'll just play by myself."

She looked up at me. At home, when I'm usually on my knees in her presence, it's easy to forget how tiny she is and that I'm almost a foot taller. "You could play with him." She pointed to someone behind me.

I turned and found a friend who I hadn't seen in several weeks standing there with a huge grin on his face. "Liam!" I said with delight and gave him a big hug. Liam is one of Mistress' play partners so I'd seen him naked often enough at parties. I do admit I have the hots for him, but Mistress doesn't permit me to have sex with anyone but her. Still, I was delighted just to have someone my own age to play golf with.

Mistress ordered pizza, paid for two mini golf games, and told them to bring the food out after we played. I enjoyed the game immensely. We got 3D glasses that made it hard to hit the ball accurately, but embellished all the black-lit pirate scenes. I beat Liam by a couple of strokes and Mistress took pictures of us with the "pirates."

After the luscious pizza, Mistress invited Liam to come to the house and visit for a bit before he drove back home -- he lives an hour and a half away. When we arrived, Mistress sent me upstairs to strip and take care of some quick chores. I came back down and saw Liam had a great big bow tied around his neck.

"You may unwrap your present now, boy." Mistress said, twirling a strand of her long, auburn hair around her finger.

I just stared at her.

"Don't you like your present?" She had a wicked glint in her green eyes.

I tilted my head to one side. "Um, what do I get to do with it?"

"Anything he will let you." Mistress smiled, but I had a hard time believing she meant I could have sex with him.

"Anything? As in I can go down on him if I want?"

"Of course."

"If I wanted him to do me, that would be okay?"

"Yes."

I almost wept for joy. "Oh, thank you, Mistress." I got down on my knees and kissed her pretty feet. "Thank you so very, very much."

My hands shook when I unbuttoned Liam's khaki shirt and unbuckled his leather belt. He works out so his pecs and abs are nice and firm. I ran my hand over his muscular chest, enjoying the feel of another man. When I pulled down his jeans and cotton boxers, his beautiful penis practically jumped into my mouth. I hadn't touched one in so long. It felt soft and smooth in my hands. The absolute exquisiteness on my tongue caused my own pecker to respond rather abruptly. I wrapped my lips around his rod and let it slide across my tongue until it hit the back of my throat. I moaned in between his thighs, and I could hear Liam sigh with pleasure. With one fist at the base of his penis and the other hand holding one of his plush cheeks, I slid him in and out of my mouth.

Pain seared across my butt. Out of the corner of my eye, I could see Mistress bringing her cane down for another strike. I winced, but I knew better than to do anything to try to avoid or deflect the blow. I concentrated on enjoying the plump succulence in my mouth, but I couldn't help a little muffled yelp when the second blow struck close on the first welt -- Mistress has a rather good aim. Liam and Mistress laughed at the same time at my distress.

Mistress handed Liam a bag of colorful, plastic clothes pins. He leaned down to attach them to my thighs, my arms, and my nipples while I kept my mouth firmly attached to his crotch. They pinched a bit, but I knew that depending on how long he left them on, they would really hurt when he removed them. When another stinging blow from Mistress' cane cut into my ass cheeks, I stopped long enough to cry out. With Liam's cock shoved deep in my throat it came out kind of gurgly. He seemed to like the sensation, though, because he grabbed my hair, and face fucked me until he jabbed the top of his crotch onto my eyes and sent warm, slightly salty cum down the back of my throat. I swallowed every drop and milked him dry until, to my surprise, he became hard and ready again.

I heard Mistress snap her fingers and I looked up to see her sitting on the sofa, her legs spread apart. I crawled over to her and kissed her feet, sucking her toes one at a time until she wiggled her rear and I could smell her arousal. Then I kissed my way up the soft skin of her plump legs, ducking under her black, ruffled skirt, until I could push aside her silk thong with my nose and dive into her luscious moistness. While I lapped up her sweet juices, Liam removed the clothes pins slowly so I fully experienced the pain of each one. I didn't let that distract me from taking care of my Mistress, though.

I felt first one and then two cold, lube-slick fingers work their way into my ass. I winced and Mistress grabbed my hair, pulling my face deeper into her warm folds. Liam slid his sheathed cock into my hole and grabbed my thighs as though they were handlebars. I squirmed in ecstasy while he banged me. I had my face smothered in the flesh between my Mistress' legs and a cock ramming the shit out of my ass. What a ride. I wished I could stroke my own hardness, but Mistress doesn't permit me to touch myself. While I enjoyed my appetizing position, I could only hope if I pleased Mistress she would eventually allow me some kind of relief.

Liam's engorged cock carved me up beyond what I'd ever experienced. Mistress' juices covered my face as she grabbed my hair and shuddered all over with one of the most intense orgasms I have ever felt from her. I guess she enjoyed watching Liam ram me while I sucked her. When I had licked up all her cum, Mistress slid down in her seat and grabbed a fistful of my hair. She pulled me up slowly so I could slide my own cock into her without escaping Liam. He grabbed my hips and drove himself into me with a fierceness that made me shudder with delight. When he pulled back, I drew out of Mistress and let his thrust push me deep inside of her. She clamped down on my cock with her muscles and I had a hard time maintaining control, but I'm not allowed to have an orgasm without her permission.

Mistress and Liam came at the same time, his bellow drowning out her ecstatic cry and his grip on my hips leaving marks on my skin. When he pulled out, Mistress finally said: "You may cum, boy."

"Thank you, Mistress!" Without Liam behind me, I could move in and out enough to finally cum, so grateful for every moment of delight she had given me. I buried my face in the pillows of Mistress' chest and enjoyed the spasms in my cock. Once my breathing became regular and my heartbeat slowed to normal, Mistress yanked my face up. "Clean up your mess, boy." I eased out of her, and knelt down so I could suck my own cum out of her. It didn't taste nearly as good as Liam's, but mixed with her juices, it wasn't bad and I got to give her another orgasm.

When she pulled my hair to let me know I could stop, I leaned my head against her thighs and wrapped my arms around her hips. "Thank you so much, Mistress, for such a wonderful birthday present. Today I had the absolutely best birthday I have ever had."

Market Boy

By I. G Frederick

Jack watched the woman in the knee-high boots picking through the heads of lettuce and bunches of beets. After paying Jennifer at the scale, she put her purchases in a canvas bag and looped it over the arm of the tall man who followed her about the market. He already had several full bags dangling on each side. At the next stall, the pesto guy displayed an array of samples. She stuck a cracker in one and tasted it. Then she scooped up another sample, turned around, and held it up to the man. He bent down to take it from her with his lips.

"Damn, that's the sexiest thing I've ever seen," Jack muttered.

George lifted another crate of carrots to restock the booth. "You're daft, mate. She's using him as a shopping cart."

"Yeah." Jack managed, barely, to keep the wistful tone out of his voice. He looked at his watch. "Hey, Jen, can I take a ciggy break now?"

She handed another customer their change. "You don't smoke."

He gave her a pleading look and she shrugged. Pulling off his apron before she could change her mind, he draped it over one of the empty bins behind the produce tables and headed off after the couple.

In addition to the boots, which looked like soft leather and were folded over at the top and buckled in the back, the woman wore tight blue jeans and a baby-blue halter top that exposed delicious breasts. He noticed a small key dangled between them. Her long, black hair was caught up in a giant banana clip. The man who followed her about the market was a foot taller than her, almost as tall as Jack himself. He had sandy brown hair that brushed his shoulders and wore a linked steel chain around his neck.

Jack followed them from one booth to another. The man stayed just a few feet behind the woman, always available when she turned to him. At the far end of the market, she purchased a filled crepe from a vendor and carried it to the table in front of the three-piece band playing bluegrass. The man held out a chair for her and waited until she nodded at the seat next to her before sitting down, piling the bags on the table in front of him. He waited while she ate about a third of the dish. Then, she pushed it toward him.

Jack could resist no longer. While the man polished off the crepe, he knelt besides the woman. "Ma'am, pardon my forwardness, but I couldn't help noticing you and your boy, and I wanted to let you know I thought it was the sexiest scene I had ever witnessed."

The look she gave him, one eyebrow raised higher than the other, could have shriveled frozen peas. "First, why in the world would I care what you think. Second, this isn't a," she raised her fingers in quote signs, "scene. This is how I live my life and your intrusion in it is most unwelcome." She stood, pushing the white plastic chair between her and Jack. "Come along, Robert. Apparently coming to this little market wasn't the best idea. We'll stick to the bigger Saturday ones in the future."

Robert scraped the rest of the sauce from the plate and

picked up all the shopping bags. He followed her back through the market, dropping plate and fork in a trash bin as he passed.

Jack swallowed. He might never get another opportunity and he had never before met someone who touched his very core the way she did. He only wanted to kneel before her and lick those beautiful boots clean. He tore after her, dodging market patrons waiting in line, standing in small groups exchanging pleasantries, and eating bagels, tacos, crepes, and berries.

By the time he caught up with the couple, they had neared the market entrance and Jack was a bit out of breath.

"Ma'am," he gasped, leaning down so he could keep his voice low and she could still hear him. "Please allow me to apologize for my inappropriate familiarity. I didn't mean to intrude. I only meant to express my admiration and to wonder if you ever might have need for a second boy whether you'd consider someone as worthless and unmannerly as myself."

She tilted her head back and laughed. The sound sent chills down his spine. "Boy, I'm not looking for toys who don't know the difference between a scene and real life or between bottoming and submitting."

"Ma'am, I can assure you that I've both bottomed and served and while the former is fun, I much prefer the latter. My previous Mistress moved to Chicago for family reasons and couldn't take me with her. I've been alone for almost a year now and would be most grateful for an opportunity to serve a Goddess such as yourself."

She frowned. "And, this is based on what? You know nothing about me."

He smiled. "True. I only know that you're an incredibly beautiful Dominant who commands the submission of this gentleman here."

With that one eyebrow still raised above the other, she looked him over from head to toe. Jack straightened and threw his shoulders back, and stood at attention. He wondered what she thought of his curly, dark red hair and muscular build. He wished he wasn't wearing worn and dirty blue jeans and a tee shirt with underarm sweat stains, but loading and unloading the truck for market in the hot July sun didn't leave one fit to meet the woman of one's dreams. If they weren't in public, he could have stripped and knelt before her for a better inspection.

"Not bad." The one eyebrow finally came level with the other. "But, I'm not exactly in the market for another submissive at the moment."

"Ma'am, if you would consider this boy worthy of even part-time service, he would be most grateful to present himself for your use any evening you desired."

"But not during the day?"

"Ma'am, I work at Intel during the week and help my cousin out with farmers' markets on Saturdays and Sundays."

"Busy boy."

"I've tried to fill the empty place my Mistress left." He shrugged. "It hasn't worked."

She sighed. "Can I find you online?"

"Yes, Ma'am. My Fetlife handle is farmboy72."

"You'd better get back to work."

Jack nodded and headed back to the booth. He turned and glimpsed her walking toward the parking lot followed by the luckiest man in the world laden with market produce in canvas bags.

$\mathcal{M}$

When Jack got home, he took a shower and dragged himself to his computer. He really wanted to just crawl into bed, but hope forced him to log in. He found a message from BeavertonDomme, but she had posted nothing about herself except that MarineVet was her submissive. His profile was blank as well.

The message read: "If you're the boy who accosted me

at the market Sunday morning, I've read your profile and I might have a use for you. I'm having some Ladies over next Saturday night and my boy could use some help with prep and serving. How early would you be available? Unless you indicate otherwise, I will assume that you won't object to anything on your fetish list, so I recommend editing it before you respond."

Jack clapped his hand over his mouth to avoid shouting and disturbing the neighbors. He responded immediately: "Oh, yes Ma'am. THANK YOU, Ma'am. The market closes at 1:30, and we usually have the truck loaded by 2:30 p.m. Give me time to run home and take a shower and I can be at your home between 3:30 and 4 p.m. Would that be satisfactory?"

He set the laptop on the coffee table, set the volume on high, and stretched out on the sofa. No sooner had he closed his eyes, than his e-mail notification beeped, but it was just a note from his sister about his niece's birthday party. He didn't bother to answer and closed his eyes again. The second time he woke, shadows enveloped him. She'd responded. He pressed his lips together and opened the message. The e-mail contained only an address and a phone number followed by: "call only if you'll arrive later than 4 p.m."

M

The next Saturday when Jack rang the bell of the two-story frame house painted silvery green, the cherrywood door seemed to open on its own. He stepped inside onto the slate entryway floor and Robert, who had been hiding behind the door, pushed it closed. The man wore only the metal chain around his neck and a steel Mistress Lori chastity tube imprisoning his pierced cock.

He pointed to a brass coat rack attached to the wall next to the door. "You can hang your clothing there, then come help me in the kitchen.

"Yes, Sir."

He scowled. "I'm no one's Sir. You may call me Robert."

Jack could have kicked himself. Great first impression. "Sorry, Robert. I meant no offense." He unbuttoned his shirt and hung it on the hook as instructed. Robert turned and disappeared down a hall to the right. After removing his slacks and underwear, Jack tucked his socks in his loafers and stuffed them under a bench on the other side of the door. Then he ventured down the hallway which opened up into an expansive kitchen with gleaming stainless steal appliances, dark granite counter tops, and a rack of steel pots hanging above the island. The smell of cooking garlic overwhelmed more subtle fragrances of mushrooms, dill, and chocolate.

Robert, who was assembling hors d'oeuvres and arranging them on silver trays, looked up when Jack entered. He pointed to an entrance at the opposite end of the kitchen. "The ladies will be here in a couple of hours. You can dust the living room and sweep the floor. You'll find what you need in there." He nodded in the direction of a small broom closet.

Jack gathered dust rags and started at one end of the room. He wasn't sure why he'd been assigned this task. Although he picked up every crystal figurine, ceramic vase, and leather encased volume, he found not one speck of dust. The lady of the house passed through the room to the kitchen and nodded at him. To his embarrassment, his cock rose to greet her. She wore a strapless black dress that clung to her figure and emphasized her curves. Her hair cascaded down her back and across her shoulders, framing her face in a luxurious sheen.

He dropped to his knees and prostrated himself as much to hide his errant cock as to demonstrate his subservience. He stayed there until the click of her high heels changed as she moved from the wood floor in the living room to the tile of the kitchen.

After he finished sweeping and put away the broom, Robert looked up from the sink where he was rinsing bowls and utensils before putting them in the dishwasher. "You can wash up in there," he pointed to a door next to the fridge, "and then get the wine glasses ready."

Jack had just emerged after making himself presentable, when he heard the doorbell ring. Female voices drifted in from the entry way and his cock rose again. He hoped he wouldn't offend the lady of the house or her guests with his excitement. By the time Robert directed him to enter the living room carrying a tray with glasses of red and white wine, seven ladies sat on the sofas and armchairs. None were as beautiful as their hostess, but he would have enjoyed serving any one of them.

After returning the tray to the kitchen, Robert sent him back out with a stack of plates and a handful of cloth napkins. Robert followed with a tray of finger sandwiches. Jack scurried back to the kitchen and brought out the tray of grapes wrapped in cheese and stuffed mushroom caps. No longer worried about spilling wine, he knelt in front of each lady to offer his tray. They picked up morsels with delicate fingers. Some of their nails had bright colored lacquer, others clear polish, but they all had seen the services of a manicurist.

He and Robert traded their trays for full ones. When all the women had sampled or declined all of the goodies Robert had prepared, the man led Jack downstairs to the basement. The narrow stairway opened into a large, carpeted room with a St. Andrew's cross, a spanking bench, a bishop's chair, and two massage tables. The far wall was covered with hooks from which hung floggers, cats, singletails, shackles, leather cuffs, various lengths of chain, and coils of rope. Jack got harder and he wondered how Robert survived with the six-inch metal tube encasing his cock.

Robert stepped over to the spanking bench. "Help me with this." He took one end and Jack the other and they carried it up the stairs to the living room. "Clear the plates."

Jack did as he was told. By the time he had all the dishes stacked in the sink and the wine glasses lined up besides it, Robert had made three more trips to the basement. A wooden drying rack, draped with toys from the dungeon, now stood next to the leather chair where the Lady of the house sat, leaning on the arm, her legs curled up besides her. She held the four leather cuffs in one hand, a blindfold and a leather collar in the other and looked directly at him. Jack knelt in front of her and held up his arms. She buckled a cuff on each wrist, the leather smooth and cool against his skin. He leaned forward and she snapped the blindfold in place, then fastened the collar around his neck. Overwhelmed, he rested his head against her knee for a moment, inhaling the scent of lavender lotion from her skin, and was grateful when she patted his curls with her free hand.

He rose and lifted first one foot then the other so she could add the ankle cuffs. Fingers curled underneath his collar and pulled him away and he found himself kneeling on the spanking bench, the cuffs on his ankles and wrists clipped to the sides, his head hanging over the end of the section where his chest rested.

Leather falls caressed his skin as someone drew a flogger over his back. She started slowly and ramped up, hitting him harder with each stroke. Jack's erection ached and he lifted his ass up towards the leather striking his rear. The thud of a thick, polished wooden paddle followed the flogger, and then the sting of a cat. For a moment, there was silence. Then long, lacquered nails scratched across the welts that had risen on his backside. He heard the snap of latex and lube-covered, gloved fingers pushed into his ass. He relaxed his sphincter and sighed with pleasure. It had been so long.

When a long, thick, plastic dildo replaced the fingers, something also pushed at his mouth. He frowned at the smell of man sweat and the soft touch of flesh, pressing his lips together. He remembered the words: "Unless you indicate otherwise, I will assume that you won't object to anything on your fetish list ..." His previous Mistress had created his profile and filled out his list. He'd never had the heart to change it. Forced bi had been one of her fantasies, although she had never found someone to force him to have sex with.

Jack took a deep breath. Six gorgeous women were watching and a seventh was pegging him. He stuck out his tongue and caressed the tip of Robert's cock. Tolerable. He opened his lips just wide enough to embrace the glans. Not something he'd ever want to do on his own. But the audience and the delicious sensation of feminine hips pushing the dildo in and out of his ass, made it pleasurable. He breathed through his nose and sucked Robert in further. Fortunately, the man didn't push, he let Jack adjust to the additional meat in his mouth.

The woman behind him pulled the dildo out with a pop and Jack whimpered. Apparently they planned to take turns, because within minutes another shape penetrated him. This one was slightly fatter and shorter than the first, but it still felt wonderful, massaging his prostrate. He distracted himself from his desperate need to come by concentrating on the mouthful of cock, running his tongue along the underside, dragging his teeth gently across the top.

Much to Jack's surprise, Robert stayed hard through all seven peggings and he worried that he might not be servicing him adequately. But the moment, the last dildo was pulled out of his ass, she said, "Give him a facial."

"Oh, yes," one of the others chimed in, clapping her hands.

"Go ahead, boy." He recognized the Lady of the house's voice.

Robert grabbed a fistful of hair on each side of his head and pumped his hips, face fucking Jack until his mouth was sore. Robert pulled out and hot jizz sprayed his face. The ladies laughed, so Jack reached out a tongue to lick it off before it could drip down his chin. His cock ached and he gasped when he felt the soft touch of lips around it. He realized they had to be Robert's, but Jack no longer cared. He was desperate to come. He bit his lip and pressed his fingernails into his palm to maintain control, waiting for permission, fighting his need for release.

He concentrated on Robert's technique rather than the wet tongue stroking his swollen prick. He yearned to let go, but he needed to show the Lady that he knew his place.

"Boy." The Lady only uttered the one word, but Jack could hear her breathing was heavy. Robert released his cock and he heard him scrambling out from underneath the spanking bench.

"Can we use your other boy?" one of the guests asked.

"Of course." The Lady was gasping for breath and Robert felt a pang of jealousy, knowing Robert must have his face buried between her legs. But moments later, he was released from the bench, his hands clipped behind his back, and he was dragged by his collar to the sofa. Still blindfolded, he responded to what he smelled, the heavenly aroma of a woman's arousal. She pulled him closer and he kissed his way up her thigh until he reached the source of the sweet musk that enveloped his senses.

Sticking out his tongue, he explored her slit, pushing into her, licking up the flowing honey until he found her nub. He wrapped his lips around it and was rewarded with a low moan. Pushing in closer, he teased it with his tongue and she pushed her hips toward him. He sucked and licked until she cried out and shuddered and someone else grabbed his collar.

Jack didn't know if Robert serviced more than his Mistress or if he had pleasured all the guests himself. Lost in the haze of subspace and a variety of sublime flavors he just kept licking and sucking whatever pussy presented itself to his mouth. Eventually, he ended up curled up on his side, his face covered in juices and dried spunk, his cock still hard as a rock, vaguely aware the party had ended and the guests were saying goodbye to their hostess.

"You're so lucky, Miranda, two pretty boys."

"And, both so obedient, I can't believe that one managed not to come."

"If you ever decide you don't want one of these, let me know. I've been looking for a third."

Jack couldn't help smile at that last comment and licked his lips to disguise his glee. Hopefully if the beautiful Lady Miranda didn't want to take him into her service, she would give his contact information to one of her lovely guests. Someone unclipped his hands, removed the cuffs, and wrapped him in a blanket.

M

After Jack and George finished unloading the truck the following Saturday, Jack dashed through the market to his car. He tore off his tee shirt, sponged himself off with a wet washrag, and pulled on a fresh button-down shirt. He made it to back to the entrance of the market in time to see Lady Miranda approaching with a collection of empty canvas bags. She smiled when she saw him and he bowed from the waist. He followed when she walked past and held out an arm whenever she turned with a full bag. By the time she finished her shopping, he had half a dozen bags dangling from each arm and balanced a flat of berry baskets in his hands. He followed her to her silver Prius and carefully arranged the bags so none of the produce would get bruised or crushed.

"Good boy." She patted his cheek. "Remember to let me know if you're going to be later than 4 p.m."

Jack kissed her fingers. "Yes, Mistress, thank you, Mistress."

The Cougar and the College Boys

By I. G Frederick

"Sorry to leave you here all on your own," Lenore tossed clothing into a worn, red leather suitcase. "But, with Chris in the hospital and Suzanne out of the country, I'm the only one who can manage the office." She zipped up the bag and pulled it off the bed. "I know I promised you time away from it all, I just didn't mean for you ..."

Tess shook her head. "Don't worry, hun. Accidents happen. I'll be fine, really. You have lots of books and, well, I've got some thinking to do."

Lenore dropped her bag and gave Tess a hug, enveloping her in the scent of lavender. "You sure you're going to be okay all by yourself?"

"Don't worry about me. I'm getting used to being alone. At least here there aren't any memories." Lenore had bought the cabin only a year before Kevin and Tess had finally parted ways and they had pretty much stopped socializing as a couple by then.

Lenore held Tess at arm's length for a moment, looking for a chink in her armor. She shook her head. "There's plenty of food and wine. The store will deliver if you give them 24 hours notice, and ..."

Tess patted Lenore's arm. "I'll be fine. I can bike into town if I need to and from what I've seen of your pantry, there's enough food here to last me a month. Go, you don't want to miss your plane, you've got at least a two-hour drive."

Lenore looked at her watch. "Crap." She hugged Tess again. "I'll only be gone a week, two tops. Suzanne's due back on the sixth." Grabbing her suitcase, purse, and car keys, she hurried out the door.

Tess watched the dust cloud disappear into the trees from the cabin's wrap around porch. When the roar of the car's engine faded in the distance, she let the silence envelop her. She shivered, not sure about staying out in the middle of nowhere by herself. But, she hadn't wanted to give Lenore any more worries -- her friend already had a cancelled vacation and a boss laid up with a broken leg and dislocated shoulder to contend with.

Crossing her arms under her breasts, Tess gripped her biceps until the sense of abandonment dissipated. She had to remind herself that Kevin, not Lenore, had abandoned her and when she recovered from his betrayal she probably would be better off. She closed her eyes and inhaled the scent of pine trees and listened to the gurgle of the brook tumbling over rocks behind the cabin. Tilting her head, she judged that she probably had several more hours of daylight. She went inside long enough to grab a key and a hat, locked the front door, and set out along the path that followed the stream.

Most of the cabins were empty -- owners usually only came up on weekends until June. But, she noticed an Explorer and a Jeep parked outside an A-frame on the opposite bank. As she approached the trestle bridge that carried the road over the brook, three men in their early twenties emerged from the A-frame and collected an aluminum pony keg, a large cardboard box with chip bags protruding from the top, and a huge blue cooler with wheels from the back of the Explorer.

"Someone's planning to party," she muttered to herself. At least the cabin was far enough away from Lenore's that the noise shouldn't invade her solitude. And, it was nice to know if she did encounter some kind of emergency, there were vehicles nearby. Tess passed the bridge and found the narrow dirt path that would take her through the trees to Lenore's cabin.

Once back inside, she flipped on the light and put the kettle on. While she waited for the water to boil, she perused the built-in bookshelf that extended the length of one wall of the cabin. Reaching to the ceiling, it was filled with hardbound copies of every best seller published in the last decade. Tess fixed herself a cup of jasmine tea and settled down with a copy of Mark Twain's autobiography.

When a series of knocks rattled the front door an hour later, Tess jumped and dropped the book. She tried to remember if she'd locked the door. Approaching cautiously, she noted the deadbolt was turned, but the transom above the solid oak was tilted inward. Listening, she heard nothing from the porch. She flipped on the light, rose up on her tiptoes, and looked through the peephole. The blond who had hefted the keg onto his shoulder as if it weighed no more than the potato chips stood on the porch, holding his empty hands out slightly from his side, palms facing her. She hesitated, then slid the chain into place before flipping the deadbolt back and cracking the door.

"Sorry to bother you, but yours seems to be the only occupied cabin within a mile of ours, Richard forgot the matches, none of us smoke, and we've no way to light our campfire," he blurted out. "Of course, we didn't figure this out until an hour after the only store in 20 miles closed for the night. I don't suppose you've any spare matches. Or a lighter?" He looked forlorn and adorable at the same time.

"Hang on, I'll check." Tess closed the door and threw the

deadbolt back before looking in the pantry. She found a full package of boxed matches and, unbolting the door, handed two through.

"Thank you SO much. You're a real party saver. I don't suppose you'd like to come join us? We've a keg of porter, we're going to roast wieners once we get the fire going, and we've got marshmallows for S'mores."

"It's just you fellows?"

"Yeah, but we're harmless. I promise. We all just graduated from University of Portland. This is our last week together before we go our separate ways." He grinned, dimples forming in his cheeks, his blue eyes sparkling. "Having you there would keep us from getting rowdy. Besides, you're a darn site easier on the eyes than my roomies."

Tess couldn't help smiling back. "Thanks for the invite, but it sounds like you fellows have a history -- I'd just be an intruding stranger."

"Ladies are never an intrusion, especially one as lovely as yourself." He put one hand in front and one hand behind his waist and bowed. "Don't say no. Why don't you think on it? Feel free to wander over anytime."

"Sure. Have fun, regardless." Tess pushed the door closed and turned the bolt. She found her place in the book, but it no longer held her interest. The temperature had dropped and she shivered. She stared at the empty fireplace, but couldn't find the motivation to move logs from the basket to the grate. Wandering into the kitchen, she pulled out a can of soup, but forgot where Lenore kept the opener. For some reason, she had a yen for hot dogs. She wondered if they had yellow mustard or if they'd brought something better.

"Don't be ridiculous, they're half your age." Tess rummaged through the kitchen drawers until she found the can opener, but then paused with the blades resting on the lid. "It would be a good way to get your mind off Kevin." But, would watching untouchable young hard bodies guzzle beer ease the ache of climbing into an empty bed every night?

Tess tossed the can opener back in the drawer, wrapped herself in a fleece jacket, grabbed a flashlight and her key, and stomped out of the cabin. She hesitated, turning the key back and forth. Finally, she drew it out with the bolt locked and followed the path toward the A-frame. The glow of their campfire lit up the yard outside the cabin and Tess turned off the flashlight to watch. Four young men sat in camp chairs around the fire talking. Not exactly a rowdy bunch. She flicked the light back on and made her way to the bridge.

When Tess entered the light of the campfire, the blond jumped up. "Fabulous. So glad you decided to join us." He pushed his chair toward her. "I'm James." He pointed to a dark skinned young man with kinky hair. "Peter."

A tall fellow with shoulder-length brown hair jumped up and bowed. "I'm Richard." The fourth, rose to his feet and towered over the rest of them. "Gerald. And, you're...?"

"Tess." A wave of male pheromones washed over her and she wondered if she'd made a mistake.

James proffered his hand and when she reached out, he lifted her fingers to his lips. "Pleased to make your acquaintance."

Each of them kissed her hand in turn. Tess relaxed and sat in the camp chair. Peter handed her a plastic cup full of dark brown liquid.

"What would you like on your dog?" Richard asked. "We've got relish, kraut, mustard, and onions."

"What kind of mustard?" Tess took a sip enjoying the delicious smoky malt smell and the complex flavor of hops.

"Beaver, of course. We stuck with local as much as we could. None of us're staying in Portland." He sounded wistful. "Horseradish or honey?"

Tess smiled. "Horseradish mustard and relish, please."

"Chips?"

She looked at the table where half a dozen open bags of different kinds of Kettle chips were spread out next to packages of graham crackers, bags of marshmallows, and a pile of chocolate bars.

"I wouldn't mind a few barbecue flavored chips, thanks."

Richard poured chips from the bag onto the plate. The chair had a cup holder, so she put her beer there to free both hands to take it from him. She watched the four fill their own plates and wondered if they'd been waiting for her or decided to have seconds. The "dog" was still hot, slightly blackened on the outside, juicy at the center. She'd never known anyone to consider bratwurst in sourdough buns "wieners," but she was soon engrossed in the bite of the horseradish contrasting with the sweet relish, both enhancing the spices and fat in the sausage.

Someone handed her a paper napkin just as a bit of juice trickled down her chin and she looked up to see Gerald smiling down at her. He dropped to a squat. "James was right, said you were hot. Why's such a pretty lady hiding up here in the woods alone?"

Tess's pulse skipped a beat and she clenched her jaw, mentally measuring how far she would have to run to get to the bridge.

"Good grief, Gerald, you're going to scare her away." Peter scooted his chair closer to hers. "Don't mind Sasquatch here, four years of college couldn't civilize 'im." He shrugged. "We only keep him around for hoops."

"Seriously," Richard stood in front of her and held the barbecue chip bag over her plate. "After we got here we just realized we missed feminine company more than we'd expected. When we saw you walking on the other side..."

James punched him in the shoulder. "Matches."

Tess laughed. They may have had more in mind than sharing their dinner, but she no longer felt threatened. They were all good looking and muscular in their tight purple tee shirts. She wondered what would happen to their camaraderie if she decided to take one back to Lenore's cabin. She handed Richard her empty plate. "Thanks, but I'm saving room for S'mores." She wiped grease and relish juice off her fingers with the napkin and opened her coat. The campfire's heat had chased the evening chill away. She shrugged her jacket off, letting it hang over the back of her chair.

Three wolf whistles caused her hands to fly to cover the low cut neckline of her form-fitting cotton top.

"Guys," James scolded. "You promised."

"We're sorry," Peter and Richard chorused together. Gerald was still staring at her figure.

"I guess all that gym time paid off." Tess had hidden from Kevin and her disintegrating marriage at the health club, often spending a couple of hours a day rotating between the aerobic equipment, circuit training, and pools.

"Most certainly." James' look had the same fire as those of his buddies.

Tess smiled, but realized it wouldn't be right to bring a strange man to Lenore's cabin and she doubted three would want to stay outside while she took one of them into their A-frame. But she hadn't had sex for, she had to stop and count, eighteen months. And they were all so gorgeous.

"The Lady asked for S'mores.." James pulled away and set out plates. Peter jumped up and laid out the graham crackers while Robert and Gerald opened chocolate bars. James handed each man a fork, keeping two for himself, and bowed to Tess, presenting her with the marshmallow bag. "Shall we compete for your," he cleared his throat, "confections?"

She laughed, pulled the bag open, and pierced two white treats on each fork. "I like mine barely toasted on the outside and gooey inside."

Peter bowed. "May the best roaster win." The four turned their forks toward the fire, carefully keeping them out of the flames. Minutes later, they each knelt before her offering plates of perfectly toasted marshmallows, the chocolate under them already melting. On second glance, she noted that Gerald's had just a tinsy bit more brown than she liked and Richard's had flattened even without the top graham cracker. She reached for that one.

"They all look wonderful, but this one seems perfect." She rewarded him with a smile. "Thank you, Richard."

The crestfallen looks on the others' faces resolved Tess'

dilemma. "I like mine with double chocolate, though. James could you get me another bar? And, I think this is going to get messy, perhaps Peter, you could get me some more napkins. Gerald, I could use a bit more beer." She really didn't need to drink anymore, but she wanted to let them know she wasn't favoring one over the other.

They scrambled to fill her requests, then stared while she lifted the gooey sandwich to her lips and sighed with pleasure as the sticky combination melted on her tongue. They'd even had sense enough to purchase dark Moonstruck chocolate instead of the more commonly used, and less satisfactory, Pennsylvania option. She closed her eyes and savored the flavor combination.

"Perfect." She licked her lips.

"Yay," Richard shouted.

Gerald mashed the top of his graham cracker onto his marshmallows so hard that all the white seeped out and he scooped it up with his fingers. The others consumed theirs with a bit more grace. Tess dragged her tongue the length of her sticky index finger. Two empty plates dropped to the ground, Gerald clutched his to his chest, and James crushed his. The fire popped and crackled while she sucked her finger into her mouth and the four gasped in unison.

This is just too easy. Of course, even though they'd only been in the woods a few hours, they'd probably been immersed in finals studies for weeks, which to a young man must seem like months if not years. She pulled her finger out with a pop and ran her tongue across first her top and then her bottom lip. Their breathing got heavier. She lowered her eyes to scan for bulges and was not disappointed.

"I hope you don't think I'm presumptuous, Tess." James voice had sunk a full octave. "But, could you let us know who you've picked? You're driving us all crazy."

Tess tilted her head and looked at him. "Why do I have to choose?"

They all gasped again.

James inched closer, wiping the sticky off his hands on his denim shorts.

She stared into his baby blues. "I'm not nearly as picky about men as I am about marshmallows, and I appreciate variety."

Peter scooted his chair closer to hers. "All of us?" His dark eyes had widened to silver dollar size.

She bit her upper lip, giving herself a second to change her mind. "Why not? You do have condoms?"

Three of them looked horrified, but Richard sprinted for the Jeep. "I do!" he shouted over his shoulder. He returned to the group moments later with a box of a dozen, still shrink wrapped, and a huge tube of scented lube.

Peter kissed the inside of her wrist. James leaned forward and licked a graham cracker crumb from just above the neckline of her shirt.

Her heart raced and her breathing grew heavy. "I assume there's a bed inside?"

Richard scooped her up into his arms and headed for the A-frame before she realized what he was doing.

"Wait."

He stopped, but didn't put her down.

"I meant with blankets ... you could bring out ... to cover the ground. If you keep the fire going ..."

Gerald ran inside and returned with his arms full of quilts and blankets. James and Peter each tossed another log on the fire then helped Gerald spread the blankets out in front of it. Richard eased down and deposited her gently. The heat of the flames washed over her, but it didn't compare to the warmth spreading from within. Peter and Richard knelt on either side of her and took her hands. One by one, Richard sucked each finger into his mouth, tantalizing her with his tongue. Peter kissed her pulse, then inched his tongue along the inside of her arm toward her elbow. Gerald sat cross legged at her feet and fumbled with the laces of her boots. James knelt at her head, leaned over and kissed her forehead.

Tess melted into the heat of male lips caressing her skin, setting her on fire. When he finally managed to pull off her socks, Gerald sucked on her toes. James had worked his way down to her neck and without removing her fingers from his mouth, Richard fumbled with the button on her jeans. Tess pushed his hands out of the way and undid them. Her jeans and panties slid down her hips and disappeared. James helped her sit up and pulled her top over her head while Peter unhooked her bra and Richard pulled it away. She heard four sharp intakes of breath as her tits fell out of the lace restraining them.

Peter and Richard lunged towards her, but then each gently lifted a breast to his lips. Peter teased her nipple with his tongue and Richard sucked adoringly at the other. Just before her eyes rolled back into her head, Tess noticed he had the most blissful expression on his face and she wondered if any of them were virgins. U of P was a Catholic school.

Gerald licked his way up her legs and Tess' hips lifted in response. Her skin burned with passion, the flames centering between her legs. Gerald's heat disappeared and she opened her eyes to see him tossed aside by James who dove between her legs and planted soft, blazing kisses on the tops of her thighs, her bush, her lips. Tess closed her eyes again and moaned. Richard and Peter continued lathering her breasts with their tongues, Gerald went back to sucking on her toes, and James buried his tongue into her slit.

She pushed her hips into his face, willing him to find her clit. His lips clamped around it and she exploded in his face. He chuckled, the vibrations teasing her further, and suckled her nub until she came again. This time when she opened her eyes, Tess realized she was surrounded by naked male bodies, their skin glistening in the firelight, their hard cocks pointing at her. James licked her juices off his lips and the tip of his nose, giving her a wide grin.

"Condoms?" she managed to whisper.

Someone presented her with the opened box and she pulled out four with the same color wrapping. Tearing the corner off one, she shuffled them in her hand and presented them fanned out, the torn corner hidden beneath her thumb. "Who wants to go first?"

Peter and Richard grabbed for condoms and looked crestfallen when the packets they selected were whole. James took one of the last two and bowed to Gerald when his also emerged intact. Gerald's eyes widened to fill half his face and his hand trembled as he reached for the remaining packet. Tess smiled at him, but he just averted his eyes. The group's virgin?

He fumbled with the packet and the rubber, his hands shaking. Tess was afraid to touch him, worried she'd terrify him. Despite his nervousness, his cock still jutted out in her direction, the swollen glans dripping precum that sparkled when it caught the fire's light.

When he finally got himself sheathed, Tess reached up. "Come here big boy. You're in for a treat."

He knelt between her legs, his green eyes dark with lust and fear. She reached up both hands and he lowered his body over her. She pulled his face toward hers with one hand behind his neck and reached down to guide his cock into her with the other. Although she opened her mouth, he pressed his lips together. Then his cockhead pushed into her cunt and he gasped. His eyes looked as if they would burst from his face before he closed them. Moaning, he eased himself deep into her folds.

Tess moved her hands to his round, firm ass, squeezing when she wanted him to pull out and pushing down to get him back inside. They'd barely gotten the rhythm established when he shouted "Oh. My. God." and lay still in her arms.

He picked up his head and seemed almost in tears. "Tess. Miss. I'm so sorry."

She kissed him. "It's okay. I'm guessing that was your first time. And, you don't have to worry about leaving me hanging -- I'm sure your roomies will pick up the slack."

Gerald started to pull out and she grabbed him around the waist. "Hold onto the condom so it doesn't spill." He did as she requested and crawled over to the far corner of the blanket.

"Do you care which of us goes next?" James knelt by her

side, running one hand softly up her leg, across her tummy to her breast.

"Any more virgins?"

James shook his head, licking his nose, reminding her what he had done to her clit with his tongue.

"Triple play?" Tess had never been with more than one man at a time and she had three gorgeous cocks presenting arms. Why not take them all at once?

"If that's your pleasure."

"Any of you experienced in anal?"

James reached for the lube. "I am." He grinned, sheathed his cock, and looked at her.

Tess tilted her head. Of the other two, Richard had the larger cock. She struggled to her knees, pointed to him, then patted the blanket in front of her. He rolled on a condom and lay on his back. She straddled his legs and turned to look at James. He nodded and she mounted Richard holding still while James splurted lube on his fingers. He rubbed some on his cock and slid first one coated finger and then a second into her ass.

He knelt behind her and caressed her ass with his dry hand. "Ready?"

She nodded, her cunt full of cock, bracing herself on her hands and knees. James worked his way in slowly, then slid in and out while Richard bucked his hips. Tess looked up at Peter and licked her lips. He sunk to his knees in front of her, his cock just out of reach. She formed an O with her mouth and he slid in, his balls barely clearing Richard's face. She moaned, unable to move, filled with delicious cock from every angle. The three gradually matched each other's rhythm so James pushed into her from behind as Peter plunged his cock deep into her mouth and Richard thrust his hips upward grinding his pubic bone against her swollen clit. They all pulled away then rammed back into her.

Peter's smooth cock caressed her tongue, filling her mouth with the taste of musk and eucalyptus and Richard and James massaged her G-Spot between them. Richard held her hips and James reached around her to squeeze her breasts. Unable to moan or call out, Tess whimpered, overwhelmed by the onslaught of fabulous sensations. The shaking started in her wrists which threatened to give way. She locked her elbows and the trembling moved from her breasts to her cunt until she spasmed from the inside out.

They moved faster and a chorus of grunts and moans emerged from their throats. Tess was still coming when one by one they exploded. She collapsed on Richard's chests until James eased out of her then slid down to her side, one breast flopped across Richard's chest, the other pressed into his side. Someone stretched out behind her, hard chest against her back, semi-rigid cock resting against her crack. The heat of male bodies combined with the glow from the campfire enveloped her.

She guessed that Gerald had rejoined the group, because she felt lips on her toes. Fingers ran through her hair and she lifted her head. A leg slid underneath to make a hairy pillow. Drifting somewhere between euphoria and sleep, she realized they wanted more. The cock against her ass was rigid and another one was pushing against her forehead. Tess tried to shake her head, but she was barely able to move it. "Can't … do … more … tonight. Tomorrow?"

"Of course." James' voice was still husky. "You just let us know when." The back of someone's fingers caressed her cheek. "You want us to take you back to your cabin?"

"Please."

Gerald carried her wrapped in one of the blankets from the A-frame. Someone extracted the key from her jeans and she sank into the sofa when he set her there.

"I'm leaving my cell number on the table in case you need us." James' breath caressed her cheek. "Just come by whenever you'd like or I can send Gerald if you don't feel like walking."

Tess managed a blissed out smile. Being single certainly had some advantages. She heard the door close, the bolt turn, and the key bounce on the floor after it dropped through the transom. "Tomorrow," she whispered.

Acknowledgements

This book would not have reached your hands without the help of many dear friends and colleagues. I thank my readers and supporters, especially Cindy, my proofreader, editor, and best friend. Thanks also to all those who have served me, well and ill, over the years. I have learned something from each one of you and I hope that you find what you seek.

Other fiction

by I.G. Frederick includes:

Complicated Couplings

Four sexy stories about tangled twosomes

"If You Love Someone" — *Tara leaves her husband to move in with Nathan, but he abandons her after a few months. When he returns, begging her to take him back, life and love look very different.*

"Commiserate" — *The same man dumped them both. When they commiserate, they discover more in common than an ex-boyfriend.*

"Passion's Price" — *Richard steals Gina's heart from three thousand miles away. But, when he moves across the country, her intensity and passion for life drive him away.*

"Lunchtime Lover" — *Both married, they started their affair with the promise never to fall in love. Then Lisa's divorce becomes final.*

www.eroticawriter.net/ComplicatedCouplings.html

Cougar Conquests

**Beautiful older women on the prowl and the
sweet young cubs captured by their allure**

"Benjamin" — A chance meeting at a munch in a tiny town leads Benjamin to an opportunity for training. But, Lady Gina tries to end the relationship rather than emotionally torture herself.

"Festival of Eros" — The handsome young man followed her around all evening, behaving like the perfect submissive ... until she learned his identity.

"Paddles" — A biker bar with no bikers? The decor, name, and patrons of a bar in a small Eastern Oregon town puzzle William who just stopped in for a beer. Then the owner introduces him to the secrets of this very special tavern.

"Starting Over" - When her pet walked out on her, she stayed away from parties because it hurt to watch other women playing with their toys. But, a friend coerces her into attending a unique event.

"The Cougar and the College Boys" — Alone in the woods, hours from Portland, Tess discovers four college friends staying in a nearby cabin. The boys invite her to share their campfire, their dinner, and ...

www.eroticawriter.net/CougarConquests.html

Dommemoir

WARNING:
This book changes women's attitudes about relationship dynamics, forever.

In Geneviéve's journey of discovery she dabbles in the BDSM lifestyle which forces her to recognize and acknowledge her true nature. Her memoir, woven together with that of a male slave, draws the reader into an intense odyssey of sexual expression triumphing over sexual repression while delivering fascinating insight about a different kind of love.

"The aptly titled Dommemoir *delivers on so many levels... It quickly sucks you in and envelopes you in the bondage of its spell...* Dommemoir *is a character study that breathes complex and compelling life into its hero, the devastating Lady Geneviéve and the fortunate submissives who worship at her feet... placing you in the delicious bondage of its dark and compelling landscape..."*

Larry Brooks, USA Today bestselling author of Darkness Bound **and** Bait and Switch

www.eroticawriter.net/Dommemoir.html

Eleanor & Mick

A journey of sexual exploration and insight

In five sizzling hot stories, Eleanor seeks refuge in a small town on the Oregon Coast and befriends her younger neighbor. He captures first her heart and then her submission, taking her on a journey of sexual exploration and insight.

"Salt for His Wounds" — When Eleanor's ex-husband shows up begging for a second chance, she asks her young, gorgeous next door neighbor for a favor and Mick takes advantage of the opportunity.

"The Mercantile" — Eleanor attributes Mick's detachment to the difference in their ages, but Mick confesses a need for kink. Afraid of losing him, Eleanor reluctantly consents to bondage and pain.

"The Things We Do for Love" — When her gorgeous girlfriend visits Eleanor on the coast, Mick's obvious attraction troubles her. But, Liz only has eyes for Eleanor.

"Paid in Full" — Mick's army buddy finds Eleanor hot and makes a deal with Mick. But, if Mick really loved Eleanor would he let another man have sex with her?

"Renovations" — After Mick spends a month renovating their garage, Eleanor discovers he built in a few surprises.

www.eroticawriter.net/EleanorMick.html

Family Dynamics

Six sultry stories exploring sexuality in Dominant/submissive liaisons

"'Aunt' Grace" — Jen needed a place to stay in Portland and turned to her father's stepsister. But, she found so much more than she ever dreamed possible with her "Aunt" Grace. Second Place, NLA:I John Preston Short Story Award.

"Leather Family" — Kyle needs his own boy. Jacques would do almost anything to find a place in a Leather Family. But, Kyle serves a female Master.

"Searching" — Two dominants love each other, but need someone who submits to them both. Just how far will young Jeremy go to serve the lovely Lady Theresa?

"Taking Control" — To free the woman she loves from a horrid sadist's perverted games, Melanie must set aside her own aversion to men.

"Family Ties" — When her slave's ex faces eviction, Katherine offers refuge. But can Naomi pay the price?

"Said the Unicorn" — Tessa dedicates herself to her Master's service, so his determination to add another woman to their family devastates her.

www.eroticawriter.net/FamilyDynamics.html

Fork In The Road:

Changing people's lives, and relationships in three pairs of sexy stories

"Said the Unicorn" — Tessa dedicates herself to her Master's service, so his determination to add another woman to their family devastates her.

"Proposals" — The evening appears perfectly arranged for him to pop the question. But, Christopher's proposition takes Geraldine on an unanticipated sexual adventure.

"Winners & Losers" — When he finally walks away from the blackjack table, Jeffrey finds someone worth gambling on.

www.eroticawriter.net/ForkinRoad.html

Ladies in Love

Six sizzling stories of Lesbian Lust

"Empty Seat" — Laura offers Alex a nightcap as thanks for help with a presentation to a prospective client. But they never order drinks.

"'Aunt' Grace" — Jen needed a place to stay in Portland and turned to her father's stepsister. But, she found so much more than she ever dreamed possible with her "Aunt" Grace. Second Place, National Leath-

er Association: International John Preston Short Story Award.

"Spa Date" — Dismayed that she introduced Sam to the woman who betrayed her, Julie tries to fix her up again.

"Taking Control" — To free the woman she loves from a horrid sadist's perverted games, Melanie must set aside her own aversion to men.

"Dental School" — How can Cindy flirt with the beautiful blonde dental instructor while her mother propositions the student examining her teeth on Cindy's behalf?

"Commiserate" — The same man dumped them both. When they commiserate, they discover more in common than an ex-boyfriend.

www.eroticawriter.net/LadiesinLove.html

Lessons Learned

Sometimes you need more than love

Four sizzling hot FemDom love stories about women who come to terms with their dominant sides and discover that makes them more attractive to the men they love.

"Tea Party" — What if the first time your best friend drags you to a FemDom "Tea Party" you see your former boyfriend serving canapes naked?

"Blind Date" — How do you respond when you find your ex-husband hanging out at the restaurant where you planned to meet your "Blind Date"?

"To Serve" — If you love a vanilla woman and you only want "To Serve," how do you introduce her to the lifestyle without scaring her away?

"Change in View" — What if a "Change in View" alters the attitude of the man you mentored so he could find his perfect Mistress?

www.eroticawriter.net/LessonsLearned.html

Love Hurts

but in a good way
five steamy stories about the dark side of love

"B&D Trainee" — Online, Xavier promised to make his B&D fantasies come true. But, had he jumped in over his head?

"Knife Play" — Seeking a knife he saw online, Jack inadvertently found himself in a room full of pain and bondage contraptions. He almost turned around and left, but a beautiful woman taught him a different way to appreciate blades.

"Pussy Whipped" — Eric knew nothing about BDSM, but purchased a ticket to a fundraiser to help out his friends. When Miranda asks him to "play," he discovers exactly what those four letters mean.

"The Auction" — He attended the auction with only one goal — to acquire a very special whip. But an offer to try it out proved irresistible and he discovered sometimes events, and women, can exceed one's expectations.

"FemDom Fairy Tale" — A FemDom's offhand remark about a photograph at an erotic art show draws a handsome man's attention. But, when two dominants find each other attractive, which one chooses to kneel?

www.eroticawriter.net/LoveHurts.html

Second Chances

Six sexy stories about getting a second shot at the gold ring

"Back to School" — An admin error forces Jordan and Dennis to share a dorm room. Older than their classmates, they decide to stick together. But Jordan's past threatens to keep them apart.

"Gordon" — When the cover model of her latest book walks into the coffee shop where she writes, Lenore embarrassingly calls him by her character's name. His reaction confounds her.

"Spa Date" — Dismayed that she introduced Sam to the

woman who betrayed her, Julie tries to fix her up again.

"Salt for His Wounds" — When Eleanor's ex-husband shows up begging for a second chance, she asks her young, gorgeous next door neighbor for a favor. Mick takes advantage of the opportunity.

"Proposal — Tangled Webs" — The evening appears perfectly arranged for him to pop the question. But, Christopher's proposition takes Geraldine on an unanticipated sexual adventure.

"Starting Over" — When her pet walked out on her, she stayed away from parties because it hurt to watch other women playing with their toys. But, a friend coerces her into attending a unique event.

www.eroticawriter.net/SecondChances.html

Young & Eager
Barely legal but hardly innocent

"Two Brothers" — A divorcée in a flashy sports car attracts the attention of two young virgin brothers visiting the "big" city of Boise.

"Teachers Pet" — Trapped at an all-girls' school in the middle of nowhere, Sabrina tries to get her hunky teacher to bust her cherry.

"Arresting Development" — *Bethany went out with Officer Rick to avoid a speeding ticket, but discovered she enjoyed getting "arrested."*

"Jail Bait" — *Serena wants Joshua to pop her cherry, but he won't touch her because of her age. When her birthday finally makes it legal, he arranges for a very special celebration.*

www.eroticawriter.net/YoungEager.html

Or visit
http://eroticawriter.net/
to find links to individual stories
and additional collections

and